MW01098701

AND SOMETIMES THEY FLY
A NOVEL

BY THE SAME AUTHOR

Winter, Spring, Summer, Fall (Illustrated by the author
  and C. Cathcart Sandiford), stories.
Attractive Forces (Illustrated by Justin Norman), graphic novel.
Stray Moonbeams (Illustrated by Justin Norman and
  Brandon Graham), graphic novel.
Sand for Snow: A Caribbean-Canadian Chronicle,
  travel memoir.
The Tree of Youth, stories.
Shouts from the Outfield (Edited with Linda M. Deane),
  cricket anthology.
Great Moves (Illustrated by Geof Isherwood), graphic novel.
Green Readings: Barbados (Edited with Linda M. Deane),
  environment anthology.
Intimacy 101: Rooms & Suites, stories.

A version of Chapter 1 appeared in *Bim: Arts for the 21st Century.*
The novel's opening scene was first glimpsed in "And Sometimes They Fly"
from *The Tree of Youth and Other Stories.*

ROBERT EDISON SANDIFORD

AND SOMETIMES THEY FLY
A NOVEL

LIVRES
DC
BOOKS

Cover illustration by Sophie Casson.
Author photograph by Carl Blenman, Studio Studio.
Book designed and typeset by Primeau Barey, Montreal.

Library and Archives Canada Cataloguing in Publication
Sandiford, Robert Edison, 1968-
And sometimes they fly / Robert Edison Sandiford.
Issued also in electronic format.
ISBN 978-1-897190-95-1 (bound).
ISBN 978-1-897190-94-4 (pbk.).
I. Title.
PS8587.A368A64 2013   C813'.54   C2013-901622-8

For our publishing activities, DC Books gratefully acknowledges the financial
support of the Canada Council for the Arts, of SODEC, and of the Government
of Canada through Canadian Heritage and the Canada Book Fund.

Canada Council   Conseil des Arts
for the Arts   du Canada

Société
de développement
des entreprises
culturelles

Québec 🏵🏵

Printed and bound in Canada by Marquis imprimeur.
Interior pages printed on FSC® certified environmentally responsible paper.
Distributed by Fitzhenry and Whiteside.

RECYCLED
Paper made from
recycled material
FSC   FSC® C103567
www.fsc.org

DC Books
PO Box 666, Station Saint-Laurent
Montreal, Quebec H4L 4V9
www.dcbooks.ca

For my sister, Shar

Based on a true story

The distance up Huntes Point didn't look so great when they left Kettle Village. Sashanna felt they could hike it in an hour or two; she heard others had. But summits, David says, are always higher than they seem, and most people are not so honest about how they reach them.

They push through lemon-grass and circe-bush, stopping only to drink or to pee. Until they stand, out of breath and holding hands, at the edge of a cliff. Looking across their parish to the one all the way to the north, where his parents were from, God rest them. Looking up, looking down. Looking at each other, sweaty and smiling.

The clouds on the horizon are the colour of pink coral and blue sand.

There are no mountains in Barbados, but that may be relative to other islands, like Grenada, Jamaica, Montserrat, or St. Lucia. Barbados has hills: Crab Hill, Horse Hill, Cave Hill, Silver Hill. Barbados has mounts: Chalky Mount, Mount Hillaby, The Mount. Sitting on their knees, David and Sashanna can see their village from here, small, small. This is how our island looks from space, David says to her, how Earth looks from another galaxy.

It takes Sashanna and him half the day to climb this chunky piece of The Rock, and it is already decided: they will not go back down until they've eaten and slept and awakened in each other's arms.

David goes to light a fire to frighten away the bats and monkeys when it gets dark. Sashanna spreads a beach towel to rest her head from the daylong heat of the sun. The towel is white with big, costumed backsides all over its front, and reads, "Bummin' it for Carnival," in bold red, white, and black. A souvenir from the only trip she has ever taken off the island, to Trinidad. She peels off her

T-shirt and tights and lies down, all in one motion, waiting for David to cover her with his towel, just a bath towel, which he does.

It is cooler at night in the country. David warms his hands over the fire as he watches over Sashanna, asleep, thinking about her hard body beneath his towel. The flames from the fire make the smooth scar across her left cheek flicker ferociously. Her short black hair is nappy from lying on it. She is so pretty–to him–like the sunset, only darker, warmer, wilder.

He loves Sashanna, though he hasn't told her this. Like many men and women he knows, whether younger or older, they are passionately inarticulate about their own intimate thoughts and feelings. David does love Sashanna, in that wordless way people on their island come to love another, but he wants to know so much more about her than how she smells after a sea-bath, the way she twists her hair at night while watching TV, or the smothered sounds she makes when they kiss. There is so much he wants her to know about him, so much he has to tell her first, before these talks of marriage and family they've been having and it's time for him to fly.

After it has dried by the fire, David slips back on his cycling suit, Caribbean blue and Olympic gold, and wraps a black kerchief around his head against the biting salt air. The stars are big and bright, closer to him than they have been in a long, long time. The wind licks up the words to an old nursery rhyme: *Sometimes, they is bright, bright, bright, Enough to blind yuh.* He walks to the edge of the cliff, looks straight down into a gully of tall coconut trees–If summits are higher than they seem, are valleys lower?–steps off the cliff, into mid-air.

He reaches out to touch the stars.

And he does.

PART 1

The best lack all conviction, while the worst
Are full of passionate intensity.

William Butler Yeats,
"The Second Coming," 1920

1

Milton sat alone at the back of De Gateway Café, sipping a rum. The television was playing above the bar, where the barmaid–Sam–tried to take orders for food and drinks as she watched with the patrons for news of the latest from New York. From New York, but also from Washington and Pennsylvania and anywhere else they might hear of across America.

"I still can't believe what them gone and do. Be Christ," said a man in a Polo shirt and gold watch seated at the bar, shaking his goatee above his drink. Milton looked at him; his name was Cooper, Cooper Johnson. "Look what them Muslims gone and do to Merica. Look what them gone and do." Milton closed his eyes, opened them. The man was a taxi driver and auto mechanic. He drove a 1993 Nissan Sunny. Forty-four. Had a wife to whom he was usually faithful and two young sons. Except he still had a weakness for Sam, who was tending the bar but cooked the food in the kitchen and had a child for him and was gap-toothed, so laughed only when he was around. Milton closed his eyes again; it was getting easier; he was becoming accustomed to the rhythm of human minds again–of these human minds. Sam, short for Samara, a combination of Samantha and Sahara concocted by her parents. Cooper got his nickname from the first car he ever owned: a 1967 Mini Cooper S. His real name was Emile.

Milton left their thoughts alone.

"Yuh see dat, my friend?" said another man. This one's name was Johnny. Milton didn't have to close his eyes now or turn his head to look even in the direction of the voice to enter the person's thoughts. Johnny Lowe was an artist who dropped into De Gateway Café when he felt for some of Sam's good food. He worked as a service station attendant part-time on Spring Garden Highway and was still in his Shell shirt. His real name wasn't Johnny; everyone knew but nobody cared, not even he. He talked like a Johnny and sometimes acted like one. His teeth were black and yellow from the cigarettes he rolled with a touch of weed for medicinal purposes, to increase his overstanding and steady his hands since they started shaking seven years ago and wouldn't stop. He hadn't picked up a paintbrush since then, either. "That is de beginning uh de end. Wunnuh don't tink Merica would go tuh war ovah dat?"

"They first got to find out who did it," said Sam, placing a plate of barbecued chicken and chips in front of Johnny beside a bottle of beer. Sam didn't like this talk of war. She liked Johnny. He didn't always have enough money for a meal, but he reminded her of her brother, tall and proud and bright until something catch hold uh he, he friends or de herb or too big plans, and he gone and lost heself somewhere in Merica, de last postcard she receive from he was from somewhere in Buffalo, New York, in Merica. But yuh never know: he could be *there,* on TV, under de rubble. So tonight Sam wished that Johnny would shut he face, stop talkin all dis talk bout war, and eat.

"Thank you," said Johnny, sniffing the food and nodding. Sam began to walk toward the kitchen. "But c'mon. Please." He reached for his beer. He was addressing his comments to no one and everyone now, a habit, Milton had noticed, some Barbadians occasionally lapsed into. "De most powerful nation in de whole planet, in de whole blasted *world*? Dem'd bomb little Buhbaydus the way dem did Grenada if they suspect any uh we did involve wid any terroris. You hear how many uh dem dead? And more tuh come? Chaa, boy," he trailed off with a whistle.

Milton watched them and the other patrons at the bar. He knew their stories. The parts that were true and the parts they made up. The parts they had discarded and those they meant to keep. He knew all their stories: the parts they believed and the parts they hoped others would, too.

Milton lowered his head. Beyond the bar, three men slammed some dominoes, one calling double six. A woman with a baby in the crook of her arm came looking for her husband, the smell of fishcakes and bakes on her greasy apron overpowering. And a boy and girl, fresh into their teens, kissed for the first time in the sea.

Milton liked rum-shops. It was the one public place where you could go in Barbados and honestly hear others think. (He had yet to try their churches.) A rum-shop often doubled or tripled as market, variety store, and town hall. He had been coming to this one, De Gateway Café, along Brighton Beach just outside of Bridgetown, below the famed "festival highway," since given form again. In quick time, he had discovered Barbadians could be a proudly reticent people, which didn't make his task of learning about them any easier, but since the news–since the beginning of the Cataclysm– their words, both spoken and unspoken, had become almost too much for Milton to bear in their shocked incoherence.

He raised his head to view the wide-screen television with a sense of inevitability. They were playing it again. At 8:46 in the morning, American Airlines Flight 11, carrying 92 people from Boston to Los Angeles, was rammed into the north tower of the World Trade Centre. By 9 o'clock, Barbados' lone television station had a live feed from the Americans. Minutes later, at 9:04 a.m., a second plane, United Airlines Flight 175, 65 passengers on board, flew into the south tower in front of the eyes of a horrified world, though there was no word to describe the emotions the sight provoked. Because no one could believe it. And yet they had watched it with their own eyes. Many thought, when they heard the news or saw reruns, that they were watching scenes from an upcoming movie. But not even Hollywood had dared such make-believe madness. At

9:32 a.m., the President of the United States called the crashes an "apparent terrorist attack on our country." A little over an hour after the first strike, at 9:51 a.m., One World Trade Centre toppled. Two World Trade Centre burned another thirty-nine minutes before following it to the ground. The Twin Towers were no more.

How many times the government station replayed these events, courtesy of its Stateside neighbour station, Milton lost count. The humans in De Gateway Café were terrified of what they saw. Yet they couldn't watch it enough. The assaulted towers, the men and women leaping hundreds of feet to their deaths to escape being burned alive, some hand-in-hand, the final collapse, the estimated thousands of lost souls. He was on his way up Cave Hill to the university when he heard the news. He immediately called in to cancel his classes.

Even he had spent the entire day at De Gateway Café, eyeing the screen and drinking his usual malt before switching to white rum. There were other plane crashes across the country, attacks on symbols of America's superior security systems. But the broadcasters kept coming back to New York, the fallen towers–for the sheer scope, the terrible hubris, the magnificent loss of life and pain. This was not supposed to be possible, though everyone knew it was. They always did. "What oft was thought...." He recalled the words from Pope, felt he must have been there when Alex penned them. Either way, he would go back to that time–

"So what's keeping you?"

Milton recognized the voice. A man dressed like him–in a cream-coloured shirtjac, taupe pants, and thick brown leather sandals–walked over from across the room.

The man was taller than Milton by a foot, and had a hard, heavy potbelly that was more muscle than fat. He had a bushy goatee, and a bramble of salt-and-pepper hair rimmed his bald head. The hair in his nostrils was black as nettles. He wore glasses whose frames made him look more severe. Milton's own hair was silver grey at the front of his head, black toward the back, and was thick as cotton wool; and he had a slight stoop, as if his bones had been sewn together in a hurry, loosely, and the flesh to cover up the hasty job, insufficient. Despite their difference in size and stature, though, they had the same sharp hazel eyes and almost grey pallor and looked roughly the same age, in their 50's. They could easily have been brothers.

"I hate it when you get like this," said the man.

"I hate it when you enter my thoughts uninvited," Milton replied.

The man motioned with his head to the empty chair at the table. Milton gestured with his hand for him to sit, if he wished.

"A rum? Since when? You better be taking water with that."

Milton didn't answer. The man said, pointing at the glass: "Go easy, Professor. You know we're more susceptible in these forms."

"I don't care," said Milton.

The man eyed him from above his glasses. "No, boy? Somehow, I suspect that's the problem. You care too much."

"After all these millennia, don't you?"

The man sat back. "I do my duty. So must you."

Milton held his glass to take a sip then slammed it back down on the table. "Why, Machiavelli?" he said, voice raised. Cooper Johnson looked his way. So did Johnny. "So many souls and more. To be lost."

The man gave Cooper and Johnny a look that said, "A little too much, eh?" before leaning over the table toward Milton. "Watch yourself. 'Mackie' will do fine. And you know I had nothing to do with *that*."

Mackie turned to the television. Milton followed his gaze.

"The fall of the towers is a sign of the times we are meant to help avert. They don't get it, Milton. I don't care how many of these so-called cosmic adjustments we endure. I doubt they ever will. Look at them."

Mackie pointed at the television screen with a blunt finger. Arabs somewhere in the Middle East were dancing in the streets, firing automatic weapons into the air, eating sweets and chanting, "God is great."

"Look at them," Mackie repeated. He stared Milton in the eyes. Both their pupils began to glow, and faintly crackle, as if the two men would clash. But the flash was no more than a spark. "Christian, Muslim, Hindu–what does it matter? They all suffer the same. Humans caused this. Humans can stop it from going any further. How are your charges coming along? Have you brought the Elect into the circle?"

Milton shot back the rest of his rum. He made a face as if his throat and tongue were on fire.

"That well, eh?" said Mackie. "Well, the Twin Towers are only the beginning. You know it is."

"I know it," said Milton. "But not if I can help it."

"Not if *you* can...? You forget your place, Milton." Mackie glanced around De Gateway Café. Johnny was rolling himself another herb-laced cigarette with crooked fingers; Cooper Johnson was ducking around back to the kitchen to see Sam, and Sam was pulling her pockets to pay for Johnny's meal. "But I shouldn't be surprised."

"What?" said Milton. "Don't lecture me."

"I would never do that. But maybe you should search your own knowledge. There was only ever one Paradise. And it was humans who were barred from its fields and hills."

Mackie stood, threw some silver coins onto the table out of an empty palm.

"Go home. Get some rest. The world will get worse before it gets better–if it gets better. But that's as much up to you as it is up to me."

2

The students were still talking after Milton had entered the lecture theatre, rested his books in a neat stack on the left corner of his desk and sat in the chair behind it, fingers folded across his chest, waiting.

It was, probably, too much to expect them to be aware of anyone or anything else the day after. Even these young West Indians were still in a state of collective shock, angry and confused. The news led the newspapers a few of them carried and the radio shows they tuned in to.

Only seventy-two of them spread across a chilled room that could hold two hundred; they filled the auditorium to capacity with the sounds of their voices spoken and unspoken. They talked and thought about New York, the Pentagon, plane crashes, overseas calls, the World Trade Centre, cellphones, the Internet, the President, Caricom, World War 3, the end of the world, bin Laden (variously pronounced as LAH-*den* or LAY-den), Muslims, God. These university students, whose education was free and whose future was largely framed in the civil service, felt very unsafe; which was, reflected Milton, a reasonable way to feel right now. These young men and women were talking everything other young men and women elsewhere in universities, probably, were talking today, often passionately, sometimes sensibly, and always loudly, whether or not they knew what they were talking about.

Milton scanned the auditorium, from face to face, the full story behind each one flashing in his mind as their lips moved and their eyes blinked and their cheeks twitched. And slowly, slowly, he smiled. He saw them. Again, as on the first day of class. They were there, all three. Engaged in their own debates, their own battles. They sat apart from each other, the strong one with Trinidadian roots, the fast one from North America, recently returned, and the one wholly from here who was now preparing to take flight.

The Elect. The Three. The Ones. One.

They glowed faintly to him, apparently of this world, if not entirely. In truth, they were all sons and daughters of the soil. Would they be loyal? he wondered, humming the rest of the verse from Barbados' national anthem.

It was when Milton heard Benn in the back row, a black Guyanese from Georgetown who was majoring in History, that he decided to stand up, sweep his books off his desk and shout, "Be quiet!" The auditorium fell silent before the books had finished scattering at the feet of the students in the front row.

Milton stepped from behind his desk, looking up as if at some imaginary point in mid-air, or beyond the room. The whole class turned to look, too.

"Repeat what you just said." Milton was talking in the direction of a tall young man with intense eyes, full lips and curly hair, yet there was no reason to believe he was talking to him specifically. It was only the second week of the semester; lecturers were not expected to know anyone yet.

"Mr. Benn," he said to the same student, "please repeat what you said to Miss Bradshaw, to your colleague, beside you."

Miss Bradshaw ever so slightly shrank away from Mr. Benn, who she was just moments ago talking to, and more for his lean good looks than his ideas. Mr. Benn hesitated. How the ass did the professor hear me from all the way back here?

"Don't mind that," snapped Milton.

"What... sir?"

"My question was clear, Mr. Benn, and you will find if you continue in this class that I don't repeat myself."

Milton paused. Mr. Benn wondered if the professor could read lips and why he had chosen to pick on him.

"I'm...," he stammered.

"Speak up."

"I–I was just saying to Termicia that I was wondering what we were doing here today... sir. After what happened in America yesterday, I guess... I guess I was feeling the way many people my–our age are feeling right now."

"Which is?" said Milton.

"Guilty. I think."

After a pause: "Why do you 'think'?" Milton said, his hazel eyes lightening around the edges. "For wanting to learn?"

"No." The question emboldened the student. "For not doing something more, more helpful... meaningful. None of this seems to matter right now."

"By 'this,' you mean Literature."

A pause, then, "Yes."

Milton held the student's gaze until it broke away from his. He turned around and walked to his desk. "I see." He raised his hands, as if conjuring, and began to speak again, in an altered tone of voice: one that did not belong to him yet was undeniably of him.

"'The satisfaction of our basic instincts is never sufficient to us. We need as people to leave our mark on paper or rock, to colour our world on canvas or with clay, to note the music of the birds and every creature that sings.... We need to refashion the rooms of our houses with our own furniture and fixtures and bric-a-brac, in images only we could dream or imagine.

"'And, most essential, we must then invite others into the houses we've built, to read our words, see our images, hear our music. We must communicate our vision of the world, an act that almost completely defines us as human beings with more than a talent for survival in common.'"

Milton looked for Mr. Benn's eyes again, but particularly for those of the Elect.

"That, Mr. Benn, is by James 'Jimmy' Weatherhead, whom we'll be studying this semester. Those words are from 'Imprimatur,' the last Faces & Spaces column he wrote for his newspaper three days before he died, swallowed by the sea, reclaimed by Nature. I want all of you not only to remember the eloquence of those words but their very essence."

No one flipped open a notebook or scrambled for paper and pen. Good, thought Milton. He finally had their attention.

"Most of you are here because you have to be. This is a required course or an elective or there was nothing else being offered that remotely interested you. This is a new course, the first time the Barbadian author, editor and Member of Parliament Jimmy Weatherhead has ever been studied at this university or any other in this way: as his own writer, not as a member of a movement or collective. This course is described in your outline as a survey of the Caribbean short story by some of its greatest practitioners and theoreticians." Milton shook his head. "Our focus will be solely on Weatherhead.

"Much of his work shares relatively few similarities with that of his contemporaries. Weatherhead was not a Naipaul or a Mittelholzer or an Austin Clarke, though he knew them all as a former editor of *Zaboka* and as a Caribbean man of letters himself. His own books are out of print; he predicted they would be even after he died. Despite an excess of modesty, he never saw his labours with a fountain pen as inconsequential."

Milton sat on his desk. He knew he held them, and had to keep them there for their own sake.

"Because they weren't. No man's works are. They can bear as much weight as he is willing to apply to them. Meaning, purpose, relevance–they all begin with the self. You want to know what we're doing here, if anything we do here can matter, particularly after yesterday's events," he said to the class. "That's up to you, all of you." Milton returned to Mr. Benn. "Our one true purpose on this planet may be to have an effect. Have you ever considered that, Mr. Benn? It would then be up to you to determine what that effect will be, how big or how small. Lamming's Caliban has had many guises in our literature, and, from time to time, not only in our literature. You should be aware of this."

Milton glanced at his scattered books. He pointed to the smallest one with an Atlee Alleyne painting for a cover. He asked a student in the front row to bring it to him.

"Next class, we start with *Mile Tree Gap,* Weatherhead's first book," he said, holding it up. "I've managed to acquire a sufficient number of copies for the bookshop. Please read the first story. No excuses." He dropped his hand with the book. "That's enough for today."

Unsure if to take the dismissal seriously, the students gradually gathered their books and bags, and then left the room.

When the last had fled, Milton walked over to the seat of the girl in the front row who handed him the book. There was a copy of one of the day's newspapers on the writing tablet, folded in half. Milton flipped the tabloid open. The front-page headline read, "TERROR RIPS US APART!" The subheadline: "If this can happen in America, the whole world is not safe."

Quite right, reflected Milton, scanning the dark copy. The world was not safe anymore again.

3

Marsha was chatting with her grandmother online when she heard a knock at her front door. Actually, she had called Nana first by telephone to ask her a question about jams. Marsha was having one of her cravings. They were usually brought on by homesickness or the stress of studying. This time, her taste was for something sugary and syrupy and a little complicated. Marsha planned to spend the night making a potful, eat it, then go to sleep. She didn't feel like textbooks, stir fry, or television. Her cravings came suddenly since starting university. She knew how to make candied gooseberries but didn't have all the ingredients. So she was consulting with the woman who raised her and had recently retired to Montreal of all places, who taught her everything she knew about cooking, sewing, praying, and love, and who saw every race she ran, attended every tournament she was in, and knew what she could use as a substitute for clove.

"Cinnamon," Nana typed back. "Naturally."

Most of what Marsha ate seemed to find its way to her feet, which were size 12, lingering only occasionally at her full hips. She was tall with light brown skin and long black hair. Steady eyes and a serene smile often softened her sharp features, but tonight she felt frazzled. After what had happened in America, she wished she were back in her grandmother's home in Tobago, where she spent long summers with an uncle–hiking and liming and gardening and training–a great uncle, Nana's only brother, who was never far from the centre of her world. Nana inherited the board and shingle family home when her great uncle died, and it was still there by the sea, like a touchstone to them both even though the old woman had traded sand for snow. Marsha needed to hear her grandmother's voice tonight. She seemed to need to hear her more and more these days. She often sensed, in the pauses between them, Nana striving to tell her something, finally, about her abilities and their origins. When the conversation veered to food, her grandmother suggested, reminding Marsha she was a pensioner, now, that they continue online. The old lady was also one of those seniors who enjoyed keeping up with the latest technology, trends, world events. After she hung up, Marsha went to the computer and logged on. It was 8:13. She remembered looking at the time on her screen because she wasn't expecting anybody, and her landlady, Miss Brathwaite, was supposed to be out of the island for the week.

"Hold on," she typed to her grandmother. "Door."

"Alright," Nana typed back.

Two things at least immediately struck Marsha as odd when she answered the door. The first was that Professor Milton was standing before her. The second was that Miss B's dogs, two unmannerly Akitas named Thunder and Lightning, were unleashed and literally eating out of his palms.

"Oh, my God," she said, hand to mouth.

"Sorry to startle you."

"I apologize," she said, "I wasn't expecting–"

"May I come in?" he said. "Without the dogs, I mean."

Marsha looked down at Thunder and Lightning. The Akita's, amazingly, obediently, sat on either side of Milton. "Of course. Step in."

Marsha pointed a finger at each dog, warning him to stay put. Don't move. But before she had the door closed they were already off to sniff another section of the yard.

What was Milton doing in Six Roads? How did he know where she lived? After today's drama in class, Marsha wasn't sure if she should have let him in or kept him on the threshold. She wasn't frightened of him physically; she had no reason to be. Professor Milton just seemed to know more about his students than would make any of them comfortable.

And why didn't the dogs bark? Miss Brathwaite kept the two for protection. Like many Bajan dogs, though, they spent their days dazed by the heat of the sun, their nights struck by the light of the moon. Thunder and Lightning were more threatening than an actual threat. But they barked whenever anybody came to the gate. Marsha had been awakened by their raucous growls at the mail lady or some boys from down the gap walking home from a fete. Miss Brathwaite–a retired nurse who returned to Barbados from Canada seven years ago after her son married and moved with his American wife to Vermont–counted on it. But Thunder and Lightning didn't bark at all. The night was beyond still. No sound of crickets or rustling palms or whistling frogs. Then why hadn't she heard the latch on the gate, rusted metal grating rusted metal?

Milton smiled at her.

Marsha smiled back, fingering the tiny silver cross around her neck.

"I would have called," he said, "but your line is busy."

"Oh. Sorry," she said, glancing behind her. "I was on the Internet. No separate line. You know, the life of a student."

"That's why I'm here. I'm having a hike with some of the students. It will be like the ones the National Trust has. Have you ever been on one of those?"

Marsha shook her head. Before she could follow it with words, he said:

"It's short notice, but we'll be a small gathering. I'm personally inviting certain students I feel would benefit from the outing–as it relates to Jimmy Weatherhead and his writings."

"Oh," she said. It was as if he had anticipated her question.

"You know, sir, I'm not part of any department... yet."

"What does that matter?" he said. "You're part of the university, aren't you? You're in my class. That makes you part of my responsibilities."

"Oh," she said again, this time surprised at his solicitude.

"We'll be hiking near or by a number of places Weatherhead wrote about. He was one for unearthing the truth in one's own land."

Again, before she could say it, he did, reading her face or mind:

"I know you don't always feel at home, here, but you really are. Aren't you?"

He seemed to be insisting. Marsha felt compelled to say, "Yes."

Milton glanced around her room. In one bookshelf were trophies hung with medals for track and field, kickboxing, tennis, wrestling. "You're obviously fit enough," he said. "Did you know Weatherhead was married to a Trinidadian? She was an actress. Some of his worthiest stories are set in that country."

"No," Marsha said. "I didn't know any of that."

"Well," said Milton, showing himself out. "I shouldn't take up any more of your time. This Saturday at 5 a.m. sharp, then."

The time caused Marsha to go pale. She was not a morning person.

"We move at dawn," said Milton from the doorway. She waved, but he was already gone.

Marsha stepped to the door and locked it. She turned the deadbolt, which she rarely did because of the dogs, which still made no noise. Milton left as quietly as he came yet like a storm. She sat at her desk in front her computer. "May as well bring in the gimp."

She glanced at the screen. Nana's status was set to offline.

4

The light from the moon shone through the partially curtained sash window onto the bed. It struck Sashanna in the face, on the side of her cheek where a thickening scar hooked her eye like a teardrop falling up, not down, as it should. Nothing about her was as it should be, reflected David, lying on his side, propped on his elbow, watching her sleep. No, he lied: nothing about her was as he expected it to be.

He met her at the auction of his parents' furniture and tools. She was a collector of antiques, what she called in a harsh dialect "dem ole-time tings." Because he had just lost Huldah and Theophilus, and because he knew so little about their larder, single-ended couch, jucking board, hammer and anvil, and wicker-back rocking chair, he enjoyed listening to someone who cared so much for his parents' few possessions. They reminded Sashanna of the woman who raised her. At the time, she still lived in the same chattel house she grew up in, along with four brothers and their various children. She called David two weeks later to invite him to another auction. "If yuh really, really interested." She seemed to be testing him, but he was attracted to her bluntness: her flat features, dark skin, knotty hair, soft fingers, and moon-shaped backside. The scar on her cheek was actually a birthmark: "Muh Tantie always say uh mark fuh somethin, doh she din know what." David liked to think that something might be him, them.

Sashanna, lying on her side facing him, had that look of perpetual worry Bajan women had. It made them look vexed, even when they were at rest or untroubled. But she slept better than he, despite the day's news. Sashanna really didn't confuse sheself, as she would put it, with terrorist bombs, once dem explode far way from Barbados. Their island was her whole world, surrounded by an ocean and a sea, separated from other islands and countries by more ocean and sea. Drive-by shootings in Silver Sands frightened her more than the attacks on the World Trade Center. Sashanna had only left the island once, for a netball tournament in Trinidad, and supposed she never would again unless David insisted they go somewhere for their honeymoon, like Jamaica or St. Vincent. That was as far as her imagination would allow her to go, it seemed.

David got up from the bed and walked to the window. He looked at the sky. The clouds were like cotton wool against a velvet luminescence. It was almost ten past eight by his watch. Not late. He began to pull on his underwear, then his pants.

Sashanna sighed in the darkness behind him. He turned. David watched the light touch her body where his hands had been an hour before.

"Where yuh goan?" she said.

"To get us something to eat. You want meat roll? I think somebody round Roy Smith sell meat rolls." His own speech loosened when he was with her like this, somehow making his tongue tender.

"You doan mind meat rolls, this time uh night?"

"No, please," she said.

"Alright, then."

She rested her head in his lap. He stroked her scarred cheek as if he were caressing a flower.

The salt air slapped David coolly in the face. He felt a little guilty about lying to Sashanna. Not lying, really, just not telling her the whole truth. Which he couldn't, anyway. He needed to get out, out of doors, into the open. He had been feeling this way day and night since September 11. It was a struggle to remain grounded when he heard what happened in America. He felt this need to break out like some caged, sharp-clawed raptor, to fly away, soar over, avenge, and protect. Sashanna thought he missed being with her and was lonely in the apartment in Sayes Court, but this feeling was the real reason he asked her not to go back up to the country this week. He wanted her near him. While many of his classmates gloated–whether from the Middle East or the West Indies, American foreign policy favoured no one except America–the whole world was, to David, in danger. He had started dreaming his parents, too, talking to Theophilus and Huldah as if they were sitting on his bed beside him. These one-sided conversations seemed to go on until fore-day morning, leaving David exhausted and late for class, though he never remembered anything he said.

David crossed Niles' Corner to Roy Smith. Just as he was entering the shop, head still down, he bumped into a man coming out. He stood back to apologize.

"Pardon me... Professor? Professor Milton?" David shielded his eyes. He seemed to be looking up at Milton against the glare of a fluorescent streetlight, though the shop was lit from within and Milton was not much taller than he. "What are you doing here?"

"Looking for you," Milton said casually, hazel eyes faintly shining. Because of the light from the shop, thought David, remarking the effect.

"I live just down the road," said David, pointing behind him.

"I know."

"I beg your pardon?"

"No need to do that. I came to invite you on a hike," continued Milton. "This Saturday at dawn. Through the mile trees straight into a gully. I want to show you students what really made Weatherhead write. Did you know he lived and worked for a time in Canada? He was a journalist. He covered politicians, mostly. Anyway, you may consider the hike part of the class work. For extra credits, if you wish."

Milton added this as David was about to say something about being busy this weekend catching up on work. He could use the extra credits to make up for his lateness.

"So we would be visiting where he wrote about, you mean?"

"Precisely," said Milton.

"What time again?"

Milton told him.

"That should be fine," said David.

"I'll see you then."

"Fine," repeated David.

Milton saluted him with a bow of the head and walked off in the direction of the nearest bus pole to the city. Except for the lingering smoky smell of a recent fogging for mosquitoes, the air had a dampness to it, like before rainfall. David watched Milton, hands behind his back and whistling to the heavens. As David entered Roy Smith, he couldn't understand why the man hadn't simply called instead of coming all this distance himself.

5

Franck slipped into the library, looking up and down the stacks and stairs. He wiped his forehead with the back of his left hand and felt instantly relieved. There weren't many students in the library tonight, which meant he could find a place to sit beneath an AC vent.

The coolness was what he came looking for, not photocopies or books, though he had palmed his copy of *Mile Tree Gap* and pocketed a couple of pens before escaping the cramped furnace he called his apartment.

Franck tossed his book onto an empty table beneath a vent. He emptied his pockets of his pens. The ballpoint and highlighter felt heavy. He kept his hair low, had the body of a swimmer, virtually hairless; still he was drenched. He sat with a huff, tugging at the bottom of his shirt to air his dripping body.

He had forgotten how hot Back Home could be.

Franck cracked open the yellowing pages of his paperback, flattening the spine with the palm of his left hand. He stared at the title story and paused after the first sentence: "For all her obvious meekness, Eliza Goddard was as shy as a gun when she opened her mouth, often set off by her many sisters and two too many brothers."

He read it again, more slowly. Its meaning only came to him as his brain cooled by degrees. He wondered how people in the Caribbean ever managed to think in this heat. It was disruptive to his whole system, which was long accustomed to Montreal winters and springs, summers and falls. It was—he checked the library's clock—eight-eleven—dark, dark outside—and still steaming hot. He couldn't wait for hurricane season to be over, and the temperate

AND SOMETIMES THEY FLY

weather of November and December. There was barely a breeze off the sea below the university, where he lived at the foot of the hill leading to it. Little moved that didn't have to in this heat.

He would get used to it. There was nothing left for him in Montreal anyway since his Aunt and Uncle died, and the plan was always for him to finish his studies Back Home. He couldn't have returned at a better time. Franck felt fortunate to be away from the US and Canada right now, after the Twin Towers' attack. The whole world was on red alert. If his Aunt and Uncle were still alive, he would have been back there in a flash, run across water.... He simply had forgotten about the heat in Barbados—and, he now thought, characters like Milton.

Throwing his books like some child throwing a tantrum. The man was mad. Franck had heard of academics committing foolish, desperate acts: lecture drunk, sleep with students, fail the bright ones out of maliciousness. Milton lacked obvious control. Franck distrusted that. The man was clearly mad: Milton the Mad.

Franck glanced up from *Mile Tree Gap*. He had felt someone enter his peripheral vision only to blot out his light.

"It's the ones with the least to lose who often prove the most gainworthy."

Franck sat back. Milton was standing before him, at ease, hands behind his back, smiling in a way Franck interpreted as condescending, wearing the same clothes he had on that morning yet looking fresh. Milton reminded Franck of Matlock: he must have had a closet full of taupe pants and cream-coloured shirtjacs the same way Andy Griffith's TV country lawyer had a closet full of light blue summer suits.

"My course is not required for you, Franck. Yet here you are, studying Jimmy Weatherhead instead of Arthur Lewis."

"Professor," Franck nodded, surprised—that Milton knew his name, that his major was Economics, that he even existed—but trying hard not to show it, to stay cool.

"How are you finding it?" said Milton.

"I've only read the first sentence."

Milton recited it from memory. "Don't worry," he said as soon as he finished. "It gets better."

Franck didn't know whether he should shrug or say something, so he simply stared at Milton.

"I'm organizing a hike this Saturday morning based on some of the places Weatherhead wrote about in his stories and essays. Did you know he wrote about New York?"

Franck stared at him. He wasn't making the connection.

"He wasn't very impressed with it. That was back in 1962. I wonder what he would say about the city now."

"Even less," said Franck, "after what's happened."

Milton smiled. "You honestly think so? I would think he would have more to say. True, it wouldn't be any more favourable, but he'd have a position. What about you, Franck?"

"Pardon me," said Franck, lost again.

"What's your position?"

"On what, sir?"

"On my hike. What else? I expect to see you there, given your commitment to the course."

"I'll try to make it, sir."

"Do more than that, Franck," said Milton, staring him in the eyes.

Franck felt his heart quicken. He started to sweat again, across his forehead and cheeks. "I'll do my best, sir."

Milton nodded. "Good, good," he said. "I'll let you get back to your reading."

Before Franck could say goodbye, Milton was gone.

Franck wiped his forehead with the back of his left hand. If he had any doubts before that Milton was mad, they were not about to disappear any time soon.

6

Daren John paused over his keyboard and glanced up from his laptop. The moon through his window was full and bright, so bright he had only his desk lamp on to type by. He was working on another monograph of the island's herptiles–its reptiles and amphibians–until he stopped in mid-sentence.

He sniffed the air. There was the damp, faintly sweaty scent of dew on the leaves, the musk of the earth. The island was in the heart of hurricane season, and the rains had drenched both pasture and gully these last three weeks. He sipped his mauby. He usually took his bitter brew of the bark very sweet, but the drink turned rancid in his mouth. He ran to the open window and spat it out. He felt the dregs at the bottom of his mug with two fingers. The flakes were coarse as sand. Then he finally heard it.

The world sounded different. The world he had been most familiar with from the time he was a bare-arsed boy running around his tribal lands in Guyana to catch lizards up to now, as a lean young man committed to the preservation of Barbados' rare wildlife, the world with which has was most in tune was out of synch, arrhythmic.

Daren listened... and what he heard in the muted sing-song of the whistling frog, in the bloated yawn of the tree lizard and clawed scratch of the leatherback turtle–the cold-blooded menagerie that lived on his family's estate with him–was all the same.

Something was changing in Nature, the world. No! Something had *already* changed. And the suddenness of the realization and the strangeness of the sounds from creatures he had up to now considered more rational than most men he knew caused him to shut his windows against the night.

Daren felt a chill and over the back of the computer chair reached for his shirt. He pulled it down over his head and left his office.

In his room, he sat in a rocking chair at the bottom of his bed. Nina was asleep with the baby beside her. He thought he would have more time. Now, such thoughts seemed foolish. He watched his wife, her long, thin hair scattered across her honey brown face. Corrie featured him, had his black hair, but her lips and nose.... He felt his son's presence as an echo of his own each time the boy's little chest rose and fell with another warm breath.

Daren had been waiting for this moment all his life. He was the first born and last hope of his people, those native to the region now called First Nation. He had been waiting–as had others in their lifetime–to play his part, in fact, to know what his role would be. He had been waiting for word from Nature, the world he knew, neither dreading the time to come nor anticipating it. Until now. Daren listened.

With a voice and heart born of the rainforest, seeking to be one–at peace–with all of Nature, Daren fell on his knees and prayed to his god as if prayers would be enough.

7

A sharp grass razored their ankles, and palm fronds slapped them in the face. Millipedes and cockroaches and insects whose names they forgot as soon as they were told crawled around their softwares, buzzed above their heads. Soiled, sweaty, still they pressed on as if on a 19th-century African expedition, or like the very first explorers to the island. They felt they had no choice.

It was only the four of them; Milton counted himself as part of the troop. This country gully seemed more overgrown than usual, even for the hurricane season. Grass and leaves were heavy with morning dew. It was like a sauna, a hot house, despite a fresh breeze that lingered on their skin. Dawn broke in strips, pastel blues, pinks, orange and yellow, the colours parting slowly, like smoke, lightening as their world was switched on again. They could hear birds chirping—black, colibri, wood dove—noisier than a body might think for so early, but could not see them in the gloom. Calling. Answering.

They were all dressed plainly, practically, for mosquitoes and centipedes. Black jeans and black T-shirt for Franck, blue jeans and blue polo shirt for David. Marsha, for some reason, chose to wear a white tank top over short crimson exercise pants. "You're not worried about being bit?" asked David. She shrugged, flipping the thin brown ponytail snaking down her back.

Milton was ahead of them, tireless, determined. For a slight old man dressed in shirtjac, long pants, and sandals, he was fit and fast. He wasn't even sweating. His clothes were no more rumpled or dingy than on any given day of class with them. He only walked with a cane, more like a branch from a miamossi tree. It was roughly four feet, the length of a sticklicker's sword, and surprisingly straight. He wielded it to cut down tall grass and bush, lashing creeping vines out of their way. He moved through the gully with an unexpected speed and strength and grace and agility that lit his eyes and almost gave his lips the semblance of a smile. He wanted them to experience more directly the land about which their class subject, Jimmy Weatherhead, was writing. More than that: he wanted them to understand something about the world they were expected to save.

Tall coconut trees lined parts of the gully walls, and above them stood sporadic rows of mile trees like sentries dressed in green and grey. Milton pointed to old plantation trails where donkeys draw-ing carriages and carts once trod. He could still see the spilt blood of runaway slaves mixed with the soil, smell the branding of dark flesh. He ignored the whizzy-whizzying of bowed mahogany and shak-shak trees where men once hanged, many black and some white, sheared of their genitals.

Milton didn't seem to mind the rest of the class had ducked his excursion, though to Marsha, David, and Franck he appeared hardly surprised at their having shown up. It only now occurred to them that this morning's outing may not have been compulsory at all. Either way, they knew, Milton would deal with the truants next class.

The only one keeping pace with him was Marsha, who didn't seem to be enjoying the hike any more than Franck or David. She was as hearty and strong as she looked: a big-boned, light-skinned girl the size of an East Indian Amazon, thought the two young men, admiring her long black hair and solid hips from the rear. Yet neither of them was actually fatigued, either. The three students were bruised but resilient. Each of them, after his own fashion, would have crossed the gully and been back home for breakfast in no time, if alone. Instead, they had to admit: Where was the challenge in that? There was something exhilarating about being dragged through this gully, being made to take each step, and at someone else's command. It was only the four of them, including Milton, and they weren't a bunch of whiners or shirkers.

At times, Milton would stop, look around him, listening, watching, feeling the air, tasting the wind. Then he would say something about the age of the trees and newness of big leaves, the poison or pleasure a particular bush could bring. "You think you know your grass?" he said, and they glanced at each other, their eyes shifty. Only one of them, Milton knew, had ever smoked cannabis, and that was a long time ago, on a foolish dare, only once, after which the body felt sick and vomited.

Despite his apparent madness—they were West Indians, after all, and the children of West Indians: they had little patience or appreciation for what politely might be termed by other cultures "eccentricities"—Milton spoke to them as if he had something significant to say, and they were meant to listen. Because he was their teacher, and because of his tone, they did.

It started to rain hard, like pebbles a drop, and the tall trees and big leaves were pelted with water.

Before they knew where to turn, Milton—dry as a biscuit—was beckoning them to where he stood in the shelter of a coral stone alcove. Then, as it often did in the island, the rain suddenly stopped. Milton stepped from under cover. In a flash of misty sunlight, the gully felt like a sauna, steamy and hot. Marsha, David, and Franck loosened whatever clothing they could, mopped their gritty necks and itchy chests with already soaked rags, rolled short sleeves, ignoring the threat of mosquitoes.

Milton told them, as they caught their breath around another bend, that Weatherhead couldn't write for a month on visiting Africa for the first time. That, in the gully, they were seeing some of what the so-called Arawaks and Caribs and other First Nation People ("The history books only know of two") saw upon landing in the island. Milton seemed to be enjoying the role of tour guide and drill sergeant. He was pushing them through the gully. Marsha stumbled over a clump of ficus roots. She fell chin first into a tangle of millipedes. She flew up, spluttering and retching. Milton was unruffled as he explained to them how harmless a millipede was. He let one fat, wormy detritivore crawl down his forearm and into the palm of his hand. "They and termites help with composting," he said, "to make a gully passable."

Over eighty-five percent of the island's surface was coral-limestone, with a thin coating of soil six times more fertile than average for the region. "When sugar was king," said Milton, "and plantations fatted themselves off its stock, Barbados was a sweet mistress. Before there were caves or what we call gullies, these channels, drained centuries ago of their underwater plants and wildlife when they rose, were coral reefs. See here, in the rock, green with moss, pitted and sharp? Remnants of sea urchins can still be dug out. All the rest is roots, vines, and trees, now. That hundred-year-old baobab is so tall and immense and regal it defies the plastic pet bottles, corn curl wrappers, and coconut husks dumped at its veined feet. This place can smell of manure one moment and then of allamandas the next."

Milton looked from face to face. Franck remained unimpressed. That one was no Nature lover. David was silent but respectful of the sky above, the earth below. Her misstep aside, Marsha was drawn to the closeness of the trees: they made her feel safe. Two out of three, thought Milton. Time to move on.

They came to a clearing in the gully. In the middle of the clearing stood a cow, black and white. She was backing them. They knew the cow was a she because she was giving birth. A calf was hanging half outside her in a transparent sac. Franck, Marsha, and David watched the burdened mother.

They each wondered what the cow was doing in the gully, how it got there. The incline was steep, dense, and rocky. There was a rope tied round the cow's neck in a makeshift collar, suggesting she belonged to someone and must have been led. But who would have brought her down here in her condition? How long had she been in labour?

David knew something about cows. His parents had kept a couple for milk and meat. He held up his arms to Marsha and Franck on either side of him. Marsha had made to advance on the cow, to comfort her. David was cautioning her not to, pointing to the emerging calf: Marsha might only make her more agitated. He needn't have worried about Franck. Fascinated by the sight, he kept his distance. The hike was one thing—he had been through rough terrain in the Laurentians. Seeing a cow drop her young a few feet from him was outside his experience and not at all what he had expected to encounter.

What was most strange, though, was that they never spoke a word to each other, merely gestured and moved their eyes. Yet they understood—knew—exactly what each other was thinking. When they stopped to question what was happening to them, the invisible link seemed to weaken, and they heard screams like the squeal of a pennywhistle.

They ran in the direction of the noise. Ahead, on the edge of the gully, they saw the back of a shackled-out chattel house sliding off its foundation of loose coral stone into the gully, dragging the front half of the house with it. There were cries coming from inside, the tearful sound of trapped children. Against torn galvanized, the shadow of a man in short pants, with one arm longer than the next, retreated behind that of another the size of a goat.

Franck was the first to the house. One moment, he was behind David and Marsha, the next, up the side of the gully. He tried to see which room the screams were coming from but couldn't tell by circling the house. David took to the air, to find a way in from above.

Marsha ploughed through the bush, smashing hard stones and heavy trees to reach beneath the foundations. She braced her shoulders underneath the back of the house and pushed up, her feet treading mud.

No good. It's no good, David thought, and he could hear her agree: If you guys have a *better* plan.... Franck quickly pointed to two, three, four thick trees–thick enough to act as a barricade. Marsha ducked from under the house, let it continue its slide down the side of the gully as she lunged for the trees. David flew through an open window on the side of the house. There wasn't much time.

The air thundered. Marsha toppled each tree with a blow. Franck guided her to stack them. David sailed out of the house, two small children in his arms. *Papa-papa.* A faint light crackled around him, Marsha, and Franck.

The house crashed against the barricade like a train wreck. They held their breath–even the children stopped crying. The house stood suspended. The barricade held.

There was the sound of one voice calling, waiting for an answer.

> *Sometimes, they does be fast,*
> *So fast you can't see them.*
>
> *Sometimes, they is strong,*
> *Stronger than a horse.*

David still hovered in the air with the children. Franck blew past Marsha, stopping a short distance from where she stood and eyeing her the way he did the cow. She was breathing hard, fierce, fists ready. They all recognized the words from the old nursery rhyme.

Well done, well done. It was only then they noticed Milton had been missing. *Swift. Selfless. Self-assured.* Praising each of them without speaking a word, he emerged from the shadows of the gully.

8

There was a loud rapping at the door. The door opened. The two women stared at each other. They were older than they looked, and they were old indeed. But now they looked even older to each other, with their wild white hair and greying skin. Felt it, too. Solid and stooped, they both walked with a cane made of miamossi. Only the carved heads were different: that of the woman still standing outside was in the shape of a black cat; the top of the stick belonging to the woman inside the doorway was crowned with a green monkey. The one outside had green eyes; the one inside had reddish-brown eyes.

"You saw it?" said the one outside.

"How could I not?" said the one inside.

From the shadows behind the one inside, another woman emerged. She looked like them but different. For one, her hair had a severe, electric part, though it was just as wild and white. And the top of her cane held a sly mongoose in place, with two tiny garnets for eyes. All three women could have been sisters, but they were not.

"We all saw it, then." The woman outside glanced behind her at Brandons Beach, at the music and laughter coming from De Gateway Café, at three young lovers in the sea, and the party-lit pirate ship offshore. She stepped inside, closed the door.

"They're here," said Black Cat.

"Arrived," Sly Mongoose corrected her. "They've always been here."

"Merely awakened," added Green Monkey. "Begun the journey."

All three of them turned to go into the front-house. Paintings, crafts, and ornaments from this century and previous ones, from this land and strange others, stuffed the narrow chattel house. At the end of every passage was a crossroad whose paths led to rooms of certain darkness. A copy of Chandler's *Slave Science* held the door to the front-house against the wind. Only the front-house was lit, with candles scented of tree oils and bush spices. It was a pepperpot of smells. They stood in the middle of the room around the light of a flame from a large, thick candle that burned neither wick nor wax.

"So it starts," said Black Cat.

"Or ends," said Green Monkey.

"Don't talk like that," said Sly Mongoose.

Green Monkey cast her good eye, the left one, up. "Like what?"

"Like any of us knows what's going to happen."

"Not even the Elders know," said Black Cat.

"But we know what *has* happened," said Green Monkey.

Sly Mongoose shook her head. "What *is* happening."

They stopped talking. There was a hum in the air, a hush in the breeze. They all thought they heard something scratch at the backdoor.

"The Elect have been found," whispered Black Cat. "Let's hope their Guardians did a good job."

"We'll know soon," said Sly Mongoose.

"In the meantime?" said Green Monkey.

"We work our obeah," said Sly Mongoose.

"And pray it will be enough, then," said Black Cat

They closed their eyes, nodded, bowed their heads, and backed away from the table, the candle, each toward a corner of the room and her wicker-back mahogany rocking chair. They sat, perched on their canes, and stared at the flame. They began to rock in alternating rhythms.

They didn't get up from their rocking for the rest of the night.

9

Milton sat on a rock overlooking the sea at Welches, near Oistins. Across the water, its beacon long dead, was the lighthouse at South Point. Wrought from iron in 1851 for London's Great Exhibition, disassembled, shipped, and resurrected the following year in Barbados, it was the oldest of the four lighthouses that stood one to a coast, like former protectors of Her Majesty's people and property. South Point's beam, generated by an oil lamp shot through prisms, once guided boats to and from these shores. Today, navigational technology called for satellites, and the town of Oistins, the site of the signing of the Barbados Charter in 1652—one of the New World's first declarations of independence—was known for its fish fries and fetes from Thursday to Saturday night. Milton could hear matches being struck, smell briquettes doused with lighter fluid burning in coal pots racked with marlin, dolphin, tuna, king fish, red snapper. Flying fish sizzled in pots of hot oil or seared over barbecue grills. He breathed in as if inhaling the greasy charred aromas.

To Milton's left, there was a door that led from the back of a beach house to the sea. Its white metal locks were salt-rusted; the door once opened onto a little wooden deck, where the owner of the beach house fished or slept in the sun. The crumbled ruins of the deck lay below the surface of the water, visible only when the tide was very low.

The door opened. Mackie walked through it, over the sea and into the air. He was sucking on a cigarette, two fingers to his lips.

"Am I late?" he said, blowing smoke with a hint of a smile.

It was a meaningless question for them, meant more to annoy than as a genuine temporal enquiry. Milton ignored Mackie's attempt at irony, though he had been waiting.

"I've made contact with the Elect," he said.

Now Mackie was annoyed. Milton was stating the obvious.

"They are strong," Milton said. "Their legends speak of a Barbadian being anywhere you travel on this planet."

"Like some sentinel or spy in every port," agreed Mackie, nodding.

"Yes," said Milton, "but I have not been able to verify this."

"I have," said Mackie. "It is true: they are strong. They usually are."

"And scared."

"They usually are," repeated Mackie. There was a pause between them.

"Everyone wants to dance in the rain, walk in the light." Milton gestured with his right hand to Oistins.

"My point exactly. This world has already begun to fade."

"Not so much that a man walking on water wouldn't be noticed," said Milton.

Mackie flicked his half-spent cigarette into the sea. "Meeting here was your idea. If you feel so uncomfortable, pick another place."

Milton stared at the sea and its shimmering surface, thought of the people at De Gateway Café; then they were there, at the back of the room, two among the crowd, their backs to the wall, as if they had always been sitting there. Before him was a fresh malt. Mackie held a beer in either hand.

"Better?" he said, raising them to his comrade.

Milton said nothing. Sam cleared two empties from their small square table. She seemed to remember him. Cooper was at the bar, eating a plate of crispy chicken wings, nothing else. Milton could sense Johnny nowhere nearby. Mackie returned to their conversation.

"Have you told the Elect who they are, or what they are expected to do?"

"Purposefully scattered, they're now together again for the first time. They've not yet asked."

"Semantics. They're too selfish to ask."

"What was true in Herodotus' time is no more true today."

"No, Milton. They *are* worse. And you mean Socrates."

"They are children, Machiavelli. That is all. As even we were once."

"That," Mackie said, tasting his beer, "was a long, long time ago."

"I've been teaching them."

"And I've been watching them. And you."

"So it *was* you who gave the chattel house a push."

Mackie looked at his comrade blankly.

"In the gully."

Mackie shook his head.

"It was reckless enough to be you."

"But it wasn't," Mackie insisted.

The Elders thought. They felt beyond the barroom and the beach and Bridgetown.

"A baccou?"

Mackie nodded. "The beasts have been let loose. There will be many more like the baccou before long. The Elect—we all—haven't much time."

Mackie downed his beer in one swallow; it was followed by a long, low, rumbling belch that shook his bushy beard. He got up to leave.

"Have one. It's on me."

"What I had the other night was enough."

Mackie smiled. "Sometimes, you take this being corporeal a little too seriously, Milton," he said.

"And sometimes, Machiavelli, I fear you don't take it seriously enough."

Mackie shook his head. He scooped up the beer and turned toward the door. He walked out completely unnoticed, as if he had not been in De Gateway Café at all.

10

"There's little remarkable about what should be, except that it isn't...." David stood in front the plaque commemorating the life and times of the first black Captain of the West Indies cricket team. "Sportsman, scholar, philosopher. 1924-1967. Dead of cancer. Tragic, young, heroic." David stared up at the monumental stumps marking the grave and nodded as he read, going over the words on the plaque as if trying to crack a code. The West Indies team hadn't been saying anything to its people in decades, not since the powerhouse days of men like the Captain. The team had become reliant on their predecessors' legacy and their own sporadic glory. How did we get from there to here? he asked, shaking his head.

David glanced over his shoulders. The night-lights turned his blue T-shirt green. Franck, Marsha, and he had agreed to meet here, in the shadow of the Captain's tomb. It was an open space overlooking the cricket pitch; above it were the pastel-coloured student residences.

They all knew the monument; they passed its towering ivory wicket every day on their way to classes or back down Cave Hill into Bridgetown. Yet none of them had felt the need to seek its refuge or meaning before tonight.

The monument loomed larger from a distance. How was that possible, standing beneath it, staring up at the two giant bails? David didn't pursue the thought. He started studying his conversation with Sashanna before he left. Their disagreements often took the form of seitus, sticklicking sparring matches: they would dance around each other, playing, throwing a cut or a lash, drawing in with a feint, trying to convince the other it would be easier–less painful–to see the matter from *this* perspective rather than *that* perspective. They had been watching a documentary on the famous speech given by Barbados' first prime minister when the island became independent. "We are willing allies of all yet will be outposts of none." Sashanna called the words bare fluff; she couldn't see how any leader in the Caribbean would get that done, in 1966 or today. With all the talk about Barbados becoming a republic, David's view was that the politicians were getting it right.

"Fuh demselves, yuh mean."

David saw the defiance prancing in her eyes. He leapt in anyway.

"There's a reason he's one of our national heroes, you know."

"Wha? Yuh tink dem words make he a hero?"

David didn't have a ready answer.

"Dem is de words of a politician," she said, "not a poet or artist."

"You saying politicians can't say great things?"

"No. Wha uh mean is dere's a difference between sayin and doin. Everyday Bajans need tuh have more pride in dey own industry."

"But the man talked about that same thing in his 'Reflection' speech—"

"Talkin pretty, pretty bout it ain't enough. Not fuh me. All our politicians a bunch uh jokers—frauds skinnin their teeth at we. There's somethin wrong wid a nation uh people who only heroes be dead ministers set barely beneath de Almighty."

She wasn't entirely right. They also had a Methodist abolitionist, a slave revolt leader, a trade unionist, but Sashanna wanted live heroes who actually did things to inspire their people today.

David looked at the floodlit field. A group of female students were playing football. It was a friendly game of kick and pass, laughing and screaming. David followed the ball from person to person, frowning. He had never been a fan of team sports. He corrected his memory: of *school* sports.

"Not flying tonight, bird boy?"

David spun around. He had expected her to walk from across the field, where he would see her.

"I came from over there." Marsha pointed up the incline, in the direction of the residences. "I have a friend who lives on one of the halls." She wore a form-fitting red cotton summer dress imprinted with small, white flowers. Her hair was tied in a tight ponytail at the back of her head. She seemed to be waiting for him to approach her, as if fearful he would take off if she came too close. What did she call him? *Bird Boy?*

"I didn't realize," David said, "when we agreed."

"I should have said something. I didn't mean to startle you."

"I think we've all been startled enough. And the semester's barely begun."

It was Franck who answered, not David, standing in the monument's western entrance. They had not heard or seen him there a moment ago, in a black tank top and shorts. He walked toward them in the centre of the monument. It was almost a week since the gully. They had been trying, as Milton advised them, to live their lives until called upon.

"Do you believe him?" Marsha spoke first.

"I believe what I saw us do in the gully. Beyond that... *based* on that—I want to believe him."

Franck gave David a hard look. "Why would you say that?"

"Because it would explain us."

"If he's telling the truth. What do we know about this guy?"

"About as much as we know about each other," said David.

"No," said Marsha. "We know more. We were all raised by men and women old enough to be our *great*-grandparents and odd enough to be carnival characters. Yours and Franck's died when you each turned eighteen."

"There's also this Montreal connection," Franck said. "Marsha's grandmother now lives there. I grew up there, and David is accepted to McGill next semester on an exchange."

"Then there's the nursery rhyme," said David. "The one the old folks taught us and Milton knew."

They chanted a verse by turns:

> *Sometimes, they does be fast,*
> *So fast you can't see them.*
>
> *Sometimes, they is strong,*
> *Stronger than a horse.*
>
> *Sometimes, they is bright, bright, bright,*
> *Enough to blind yuh.*
>
> *And sometimes they does fly.*
>
> *No one knows why they born or to who*
> *But as they are, they must be true.*
>
> *So sometimes they does be feared, too.*

"I had those words drummed into my skull from the time I was eight or nine, same as the rest of you," Franck said. "I thought it was a cautionary tale, warning me not to let others know I was different. Now, I'm supposed to believe it's an apocalyptic verse?"

Franck's voice echoed slightly in the vaulted space, and Marsha and David looked up and around them. The girl's football team was packing up their gear, the softly lit campus was quiet. Except Marsha had an uneasy feeling when she glanced up at the roof of the residences.

David read her. "What's wrong?"

Instinctively, she replied without speaking. "I thought I saw someone on the roof."

"Where?"

She directed Franck to the nearest building, but there was no one on the roof.

David drew them back to him. He could sense their fear, and it was now making *him* nervous.

"There are too many coincidences," he said. "Milton. We have to talk to Milton."

Franck agreed, and so did Marsha. Franck felt Milton couldn't tell them any more foolishness than he already had. Marsha kept eyeing the rooftops of the residences. She saw nothing.

11

He saw the beast, then the beast was gone: peeking over the gutters at the Elect, its bald head a pale pink in the moonlight, tufted with white hairs, wide eyes like hot coals in coarse sand–then out of sight–disappeared down the side of the residence by the time Daren reached. Daren had kept watch from the ground as he tracked the beast known for its fondness for galvanized roofs, rockstones, and mayhem.

This was the second time the beast had slipped him. It was as agile hopping from rooftop to rooftop as it was swinging from vine to vine in a gully.

Daren sheathed his sword and rested his haversack on the ground. He felt inside the bag for the Plexiglas netting. A glass cage was best, but this acrylic would do.

The beast must have spotted him. Its large lidless eyes gave it the ability to see everything around it without turning its head much.

Daren stared at his bag. He anticipated the beast–what he didn't anticipate was its spying on the Elect. It showed sense. Only the girl seemed aware of its presence.

The Elect looked so young. That surprised Daren, too.

Until the Cataclysm, he didn't know they or the baccou on the roof could exist in reality. He knew how to catch a baccou; because it was a creature of Caribbean legend and myth, there were many tales about how to track and tame the beast. But he didn't know what he should do if the baccou attacked the Elect. Daren wasn't permitted to reveal his presence. Not unless the island was overrun, and he prayed to his ancestors it would not come to that.

The ruddy beast looked almost harmless in ragged pants, like a gnome or walking pig on its way to the beach. It seemed to be only watching. The Elect did not look prepared. They sounded uncertain. From how they talked, Daren thought, it was as if they knew as much as he did about the way the world was now turning and their role in its revolutions.

Daren slung the haversack over his shoulder. He stared at the shadowy field of the university campus; traffic moved slowly under the bright lights beyond its boundaries.

It was almost nine o'clock, a sleepy hour in the island. The Change was becoming more magnetic. The baccou's presence was proof of that.

12

Marsha sat in the dark, her hands in her lap, in front her computer screen. She tried calling Nana as soon as she got in. She had felt anxious all night–all day–and couldn't explain why. She understood when she met with David and Franck, and heard their stories.

David's parents and Franck's uncle and aunt, the men and women who raised them, died on their eighteenth birthdays. Her classmates assumed that Marsha was eighteen and her grandmother had somehow been spared. Marsha wasn't eighteen. Her birthday was in October. She entered school, as did many children born late in the calendar, a year early.

If the events of their lives were more than coincidence, then Nana had only weeks to live. Marsha glared at her inbox. Every message to Nana–those sent throughout the day and since her return from the university tonight–had bounced back. The telephone line was not in service when Marsha tried to call. That might explain the online silence, the returned emails, not Nana's total absence.

Marsha wanted to pelt her monitor across the living room and through the window. She was not accustomed to feeling helpless. She always had enough strength for any situation she found herself in. Like that time she was seven, and she and her grandmother were in Tobago and the hurricane struck. They were visiting her great uncle. Her grandmother refused to leave her brother alone to suffer the storm, though he seemed undisturbed by its passing. Very different personalities, their one unifying feature was the curly red hair that framed their faces. Marsha was standing in the living room looking out into the swirling rain at the bent royal palms and swaying samaans when she heard the wind roar, then nothing, perfect silence, before a minivan spun into the room in a comet of broken glass and duct tape. Her grandmother screamed, her great uncle, a moment ago so placid, screamed. Marsha's hands shot out to catch the flying vehicle. Glass shattered against her arms and chest. She leaned into the storm now raging inside the house. She held the minivan over her shoulders, away from her grandmother and great uncle, until she was sure they were safe and they told her where to rest it.

She always had enough strength. Whatever the challenge, she was never scared. Except this time she didn't know who or what she was fighting. She couldn't see it coming at her, though she could feel it. And because she could feel it, unlike the broken glass from the crashed living room window or the twisted metal of the minivan, she was beginning to understand the meaning of fear. It was when you realized you might not be invulnerable after all.

Marsha searched the bright screen. A cold sweat streamed down her back. Another new sensation seized her. Nana was no longer out there, within reach, at the other end of some line that kept them both grounded. For the first time she could remember, Marsha was truly on her own.

13

The old obeah woman sprang to her feet. The wicker-back mahogany rocking chair in which she sat by the light of a single candle went spinning behind her. It crashed against a wall without breaking.

Her eyes were wide and watery. She struggled with her visions, their emotions.

Black Cat opened her mouth in a drum-piercing screech.

The other two obeah women–Green Monkey and Sly Mongoose–bolted upright, screaming in chorus with their sister.

"She's gone," said Black Cat.

"The last of the Guardians," said Green Monkey.

"Masking sheself from us and she child," said Sly Mongoose.

"This is not good," said Black Cat.

"At all, at all," said Green Monkey.

"What to do?" said Sly Mongoose.

"Something," said Black Cat.

"If we can't find her–" said Green Monkey

"Bring she back–for the sake of she child–for the sake of–" said Sly Mongoose.

Green Monkey looked most disturbed. Since the last time, she always did. Sly Mongoose was the oldest of the Three Who Look Like One. She had lived the most and suffered the most. But Black Cat was the only one who knew what it was like to be defenceless, born to die. She embraced her sisters into a huddle, to commune. Their arms reached round each other, their clouded eyes toward the sky.

14

David, Franck, and Marsha sat together in the middle of the room, a short distance from Milton. Arms folded, they were the only three students left in the cold auditorium. The class drained fast when Milton pulled the plug. Nobody noticed they stayed behind. Milton didn't invite after-hours consultations, insisting to students whatever reassurance they sought was to be found either in the stories they studied or their own efforts. He repeatedly challenged them to be more than lazy readers, unimaginative thinkers.

In this one respect, he was like the rest of their professors. In all others, his students regarded him as uncommon, odd, and menacing, not just intimidating as some academics could be.

Every one of Milton's students had been attentive today, alert to his questions and their own, except the Elect. He doubted they remembered the assignment he gave, if they even took it down. He had opened his thoughts to theirs, briefly; he didn't like to do this to humans or other beings because he simply could. Their minds were in riot, confused and confusing.

It had been a good lecture on Weatherhead's "Lean Streets."

"The work of any of the writers listed in your outline could fill an entire course," Milton told them, "all two semesters. Wouldn't you agree?"

This was already one of his obvious tactics: putting the question to them instead.

"All of Weatherhead's writings are dark, in one way or another—they deal with despair. In 'Lean Streets,' we see the author's sympathy for humanity's situation, as experienced by young people such as yourselves, and his understanding of his people—their character as represented by the girl in the story. Note his eye for detail, his passion for description, his careful use of language. What's he showing us about our society?"

"That it's a hellish place," someone said from the back of the class.

"It can be. It has been," Milton allowed. "And now? Is this story still valid?" A hand went up. "Yes?"

"Well, to me, sir, there's something about Weatherhead's end that may help us to understand what he's trying to say in this story better."

Milton nodded. "Go on. What have we discovered so far about him and ourselves?"

"Well, sir," the student said, "maybe that you can lead a man to the sea, but you can't make him swim."

There were English Lit majors, students from other faculties or departments who signed up for this class because they liked to read or were good at book reports back in secondary school or they thought analyzing the words of West Indian writers was easier than solving a calculus problem or designing a bridge. Most of the class had been stuffed with British literature (and not even the best of it), if they had been fed with words at all, and knew very, very little, actually, about their own writers and their ideas.

"Maybe," Milton said. "In light of what has happened in the world today, *to* the world today, I would say it's vital we take another look at what our most valuable prophets have been telling us, don't you?"

Only a few weeks into class, they were uncomfortably intimate with Milton's style of attack. No one answered, yet it was not entirely rhetorical.

Someone shot back, without raising a hand and as Milton turned to pick up his shackled-out copy of *Revelations*: "But what does de bombin of Merican buildings by a hanful uh Moslems have tuh do wid we?"

"Awright, then," came another, also unsolicited.

Milton spun in the direction of the voices. They echoed from the back—they usually did—to his right. He stared in that corner, took two steps forward. Within a moment—the time was immeasurably short—he was staring directly at the boy who had spoken first and also at a girl beside him. It was as if a spotlight had been beamed onto his knotty head and her tight locks. They had started to sleep together recently, which explained their current solidarity. Milton didn't need to probe any further into their thoughts.

"A couple weeks from now, V. S. Naipaul, being V. S. Naipaul, will call the events of September 11 'astonishing,' 'one of a kind,' assuring his audience in America, in the city where this Cataclysm took place, that 'it can't happen again.' He is wrong. It has happened before, to humanity and to other *peoples*. It will happen again. Many times over. Sir Vidiadhar is *wrong*."

No one knew what to say to this; Milton often spoke with an almost ancient authority that devastated arguments to the contrary before they could be uttered.

"I was only saying...." The boy trailed off.

The girl kept quiet.

The spotlight dimmed. Milton stepped back. For a man who looked the definition of meek when at rest, Milton gave his students the impression he had flown through suns and lived many lives. He raised the book in his hand; *Revelations* was coming undone leaf by leaf. "Ignore the production values—Weatherhead deserved better handlers in publishers and printers. It's his *words* we're after, and all the ones we want are here. Admittedly, they will be in the sombre stories, those that lean toward a Caribbean noir aesthetic that is symbolic and speculative. As in Naipaul, there is an appreciation of the power of cumulative, carefully chosen minutia to craft the Truth about humanity. That Beauty may be unearthed in a dung heap."

15

Now class was over, and Milton was attempting to tell David, Franck, and Marsha as much as he could about their situation; they quietly formed a line of resistance. He hadn't expected such denial, not after the way they worked together in the gully and what they had learned about each other since.

"What are we?" asked David.

"You are the Elect. The men and women you knew as parents, grandparents, aunt and uncle, were your Guardians, charged with the special task of guiding and protecting you all their lives until you were ready."

"So what are you?" said Marsha, concealing the briefest of smiles.

"I am an Elder. It is the only name I have ever known for myself, my kind. And it is my duty, and that of another, to shepherd you three to your final purpose...."

Milton hesitated. He saw the looks on their faces, especially Franck's. Yes, he supposed it was all rather much to take in, even with the gully. They were still students, despite their great power and responsibility. Until this moment, their clearest challenge in life had been what they would do after graduation in three or four years.

"This is bare shite!" said Franck. He got out of his seat. Milton felt the boy's words–and fear–before he spoke them. He sensed David and Marsha were not entirely disbelieving, but Franck was far from convinced.

"I've wondered all my life if my abilities were for me alone," said David, staring at Milton.

Franck looked around. "You believe him? The man's mad."

"Do you believe I can fly? Or that Marsha's stronger than Wonder Woman?"

"That's different," he said.

"Or *connected*. Is it?" David said to Milton. The Elder didn't answer.

Marsha rose toward Franck. "I want to hear what more he can tell us," she said. "Three weeks ago, none of us knew about each other; we were like The Breakfast Club. Now we do, and Nana—my grandmother—is missing."

"And you think it has something to do with *him*?" Franck pointed at Milton.

"It could.... I don't know...."

Franck settled back in his seat. He became aware of Marsha's concern and David's composure.

"This must be some Lodge trick," he said.

Milton raised his eyebrows. "What would Barbados' Sacred Order of Freemasons have to do with this?"

"You tell me," Franck said.

"Nothing that I know of. Although I'm sure they'd like you to believe differently. They and their fellow constitutions, the Circle of the Grand Order, have stood outside our design for some time. Those of the inner column who lead them are more secret than sacred these days."

"So... you're an angel, then?" said Marsha.

Milton was again surprised. In all his ages, in all the peoples he had dealings with, he had never encountered such resistance as he had from these so-called Bajans! For a reputedly intrepid tribe, they were sceptical.

"Not quite," he replied. "In fact, no.... How best to explain it? I see what you're asking me—and why. I can only tell you I am what I have always known myself to be, which is what I have described myself as: an Elder."

"And what do you want with us?" said David. "I mean, why us? Why should we believe we're so special?"

Milton seemed to look at all of them–all three of them–at once. "Because you *are*. And you must fulfill your purpose. It is your time to fight for this world."

He was straight-faced. They didn't know what to say. But they all thought it at once: Milton must be mad, after all.

"So... we fight, we win–"

"If you win–" he said to Marsha.

"*If* we win... what then? What happens?"

Milton remained silent.

"I mean, we live, we die, we walk away...?" said Marsha.

"Yes," said Milton.

"Yes?" repeated Franck. "To which one?"

"To all," said Milton, narrowing his eyes. "We each have our time: your Guardians, we Elders.... You should have been prepared for this. It's in the verse you were all taught:

And where they go,
On the other side,
No one follows
Or ever returns."

Marsha, David, and Franck glanced at each other.

"I've never heard that part of the poem," said David. "Have you?"

Both Franck and Marsha shook their heads.

Milton rubbed his smouldering eyes with the tips of his fingers. "They never told you," he said. He exhaled softly. "They must have cared for you all... too greatly."

16

Franck marched through the hall to the courtyard, muttering to himself but trying hard to keep it down. He didn't like to get angry in public, and he hated even less that habit Barbadians had of complaining to themselves just above a whisper (sometimes louder) when upset. It was that loss of control he disliked most. Yet he couldn't stop himself from ranting, if only under his breath. What he was saying he'd definitely want to keep to himself, anyway. People would think he was mad, cart him off to the psychiatric hospital just down the hill.... No. Milton was insane.

"Who put him up to this?" Franck cuffed a locker in passing, so fast students heard the metallic ping as he rushed by but never saw what caused it.

And why was he so convinced this had something to do with the Lodge?

Franck didn't care what he had heard or seen in the last few days. He refused to buy whatever flavour Kool-Aid Milton was selling. He didn't object when Milton told them what he and the others were or how they came to be. He had experiences and abilities that needed explaining. One lie would do as well as another. But to save the world? Bad things happened to people all the time, throughout time. How was the crashing of the World Trade Center any worse than the Crusades, or the Inquisition, or the Atlantic Slave Trade, or the Holocaust, or all the world wars totalled?

It wasn't. It couldn't be.

Within seconds, Franck was on the outskirts of the wide, green campus, by the cricket pavilion, not far from the Captain's tomb, where he, David, and Marsha met. His feet had taken him. They always did.

He was only seven or eight when he realized he could run like The Flash: faster than sound, a bullet, probably even light, though he had not attempted that. He was unsure what would happen to him if he ran that fast. What he knew for sure was that he was always as fast as he needed to be.

A gang of French kids from his school tried to beat him up one time at lunch. They were led by a boy named Alain. Franck knew Alain was dangerous. He was one of those kids who was always trying to show how brave he was. Dangerous. At first, Franck hid in the principal's office. She told the little punks to go home and eat. When they wouldn't listen, she went back to her office and sat. She stared at the wooden meter-long ruler on her desk, muttering, "Quoi faire, quoi faire?" Fed up, Franck decided it was time to leave.

The boys came out from behind two snow banks pelting snowballs studded with bits of gravel. He ran; they ran after him. They were all young, angry, and fast. Except every time one got close to him, he got faster. They couldn't catch him. After that day, no one ever did.

His Aunt and Uncle warned him about fighting, especially in high school, when he would often test himself. They were afraid he might hurt someone—with an accelerated punch that could crack a skull or cause internal injuries. His Aunt and Uncle weren't what he would call warm, but they were caring. They often opened their doors to West Indian immigrants.

Bart was one of them: a white Bajan, a Lodge member, and a drunk. He would come home from a meeting in NDG still dressed in his purple and gold sash, carrying a decorated bag, and already fired up. He was sworn to secrecy but likely to talk about anything with a few rums in him. Franck's Aunt and Uncle listened patiently, as if they never had anywhere to go or anything to do, no matter how early or late he returned. Bart talked most about

Lodge rituals, what they were really like or resembled, flashing the gold onyx pinky ring with the compass and right angle ruler on his left hand. The symbols formed a sticklicker's training diamond.

Franck's Aunt and Uncle once brought out the rum to keep Bart talking at the table. Something was up. They were attentive whenever Bart talked, but never enthusiastic. His Aunt put a shot glass on the table; his Uncle broke the seal on a fresh bottle. VSO, it was all they ever stocked, though they never drank anything stronger than ginger beer. His Aunt and Uncle took turns pouring for Bart. Both nodded their heads: matching crops of wispy white hair with a bolt of red bouncing up and down the middle. Words flowed out of Bart with the liquor, and he forever seemed to be coming to some revelation, on the verge of making His Point, only to fall back into his seat again, to crash again. Talk of a New World Order, the problem with The System, the End of Days. His Aunt and Uncle seemed to be trying to get him to confess to something, something the rum was supposed to make it easier to unload. Pour. Drink. More talk. His Aunt and Uncle, caring but reserved, said more during those post-Lodge-meeting sessions with Bart than Franck had ever heard them say to anyone else, except maybe to himself. He couldn't remember a clear conversation; he wasn't so fascinated by what Bart had to say, though he had gotten the feeling Bart was never as drunk as he seemed when he left the table searching for the bathroom and his bed.

Bart was not related to them. Franck couldn't clearly remember how the man came to live in their house for so long. But what kept them all together seemed to be a secret that had to do with Back Home, unspeakable tragedy, and the Lodge.

Afterward, when Bart stumbled upstairs, Franck dashed up behind him. He wanted to see what Bart did with his sash and ring when he took them off, where he hid them. Bart's door was open a crack. When Franck peeped in, Bart was knelt over a shiny mahogany box he had never seen before. Was it in his closet, which was always kept locked? It was too big to slide under the bed. Franck's heart started to beat faster; he could hear its pounding in his ears, smell its blood in his nostrils. Bart removed his sash and ring and rested them neatly beside a lit oil lamp, the kind old miners used. The noise in Franck's ears echoed inside the box (or was it the other way round?), and raced to a beat that was at first steady and precise, then galloping and erratic: papa-papa, papa-papa. Seams of the mahogany box leaked a jaundice light, like parched leaves dripping sun.

A loud bell clanged, and people ran past him. Students and faculty went screaming down the winding drive to the campus into oncoming traffic. It took Franck a moment to focus. He thought it was another bomb scare, this time for real. There had been two for the semester already, out of season; midterm exams were weeks away, when desperate students would turn foolish.

Franck doubled back toward the auditorium.

He almost stumbled and fell at the evergreen tree across from the bookshop. Tearing up the pasture like a rhinoceros was a huge, fire-snorting, armoured donkey.

The juggernaut of a beast trotted to a stop when it saw Franck. Its body made a clanging when it moved its heavy hooves, and another sound followed its charge, like a tuk band of hammers on anvils and pokers stoking fires and pliers bending metal. There was a charcoal smell of coal pot smoke in the air. Ogun, Franck thought, yet the donkey was not ridden by the Yoruba god of iron and war. He had never seen an animal this big and fast, not even a moose. Its armour was a tinpan mix of dusty red, brown, and black galvanized sheeting. Its head was covered, except for its smoky blue eyes. One was larger than the next, wilder.

Both locked on him and narrowed. There was intelligence in the gaze–recognition. In an instant, faster than Franck could think to run, the steel donkey had ploughed through him. The beast's front hooves caught him in the ribs, and Franck was thrown against the evergreen. Two ribs cracked, on his left; the pain was electric. He slid to the ground, stunned and crumpled.

Like a matador thrown off his feet, Franck willed himself to stand. To get up and run. Run fast.

He got no further than the thought.

The beast reared. Snorting fire, it turned around. Smoky eyes. Cruel. Franck could hear his heart beating, thumping against his chest in a way it never did even when he ran on water. Except that time outside Bart's door, when there was a ruction like this, and suffocating heat, and a savage smell of blood. There was the sound of a hundred hearts beating, before a hand with a sword shut the door and the house's walls collapsed and their painted panels went blank.

End of Part 1

PART 2

Our deepest fear is not that we are inadequate.
Our deepest fear is that we are powerful beyond measure.
It is our light, not our darkness, that most frightens us.

Marianne Williamson, *A Return to Love*, 1992

17

Daren sat at the small, round table in his kitchen, sipping his morning tea. It was brewed from a mixture of bay leaves, fresh ginger, and mint, meant to help open his senses, clear his mind. There was a dryness to the air outside, a brittleness to the leaves on the tress, that was familiar during hurricane season. Still heat, lazy wind, and shiny skies were the calming signs seen hours ahead of a storm. But it had been this way for most of October, and neither tropical storm nor hurricane had approached Barbados. Since September 11, they all steered in opposite directions.

Daren thumbed the carvings of his calabash mug. He rested the mug on the table beside the newspapers. He had the two tabloids side by side. One's lead back-page story was the other's front-page story. Both headlines alluded to a "steel donkey rampage" at the university. There were pictures of students–children–crying and holding each other, dazed, terrified looks on their faces. Neither newspaper had a picture of the beast that caused the mayhem on campus the day before. The reporters who filed the stories said those attacked described the beast as a giant steel donkey. "De most hellish thing I did ever see in muh life," said one girl. The reporters speculated: "More likely, the rampage was caused by a large bull cow. A young man dressed in khaki cargo shorts, who was not believed to be a student enrolled at the university, chased the animal away with a stick when it was about to trample a student." The Samaritan could not be found to thank afterward, nor the beast. The student was in the hospital recovering from his injuries. With uncommon irony for local papers, the article ended: "There were no reports of baccous or djablèses roaming the area." Inside the newspapers were further stories on America. That nation was attempting to find its footing. The rest of the world watched, also still in shock.

Daren caressed the grooves of the cooling calabash, feeling the ridges ripple beneath his touch. And now there are two? he thought.

"I am the Elect's first defence against the return of the beasts," he said to Nina. She had been warming the baby's bottle while Daren read. She and Daren wanted Corrie to breastfeed, but Nina's milk dried up within days of bringing him home.

Nina rubbed the nipple against his lips. "You were out hunting the baccou. You can't be everywhere at once."

"But I did not catch him." Daren looked up from the headlines. "And there should be no need for this other Protector."

"You should be happy for the help," she said, rocking Corrie on her lap as he sucked from the bottle.

"I am," he said. He could tell he had surprised her. He had surprised himself, too, a little. He was the leader of their people and one of a select circle ever entrusted with such a mission, yet he was not trained to be proud foolish. "Even if this means the situation is no closer to being decided."

The baccou had eluded him in the country, near the island's first free village. The beast was mocking him, showing him how easy it could disappear. It shelled with stones the galvanized roofs of nine chattel houses, all in a row, and with its claws slit the throats of three goats from three different pastures before going to ground in a gully. What lurked in a gully often stayed in a gully, but once whispered by Nature into being, it needed food and water and rest, just like him. He would have to go in and root it out before it became deeply entrenched in the earth and more dangerous.

"The Elect in hospital will recover, then?" Nina said.

"From what the matron told me, yes. This time."

"And how much time do they all have until they must meet the Others?"

"Until the Winter Solstice." If that long, he thought but didn't say.

In truth, Daren was grateful for the assistance of this second Protector. The Elect were not harmed–that was all that mattered. What troubled him was how quickly after the baccou the steel donkey was summoned. There were no set intervals for their appearance. They could be realized anytime, anywhere, their existence and number entirely dependent on the Elect's clarity of purpose.

Daren took a sip from his calabash, watched his wife feed their child. Why had Nina's milk dried up? He grew cold in the flat heat of the day. If the Elect did not decide soon, the beasts would be everywhere and their burdens everyone's.

18

Marsha stood at the foot of Franck's bed. He was asleep when she came in, and she was warned by the nurse not to disturb him.

"You his girlfriend? Not a relative? You can stay but don't disturb he. Poor boy been through nuff with that 'steel donkey' went mad." Marsha didn't respond. The woman was friendly enough but maco–Marsha was East Indian, had a Trini lilt to her Bajan accent, and was taller than Franck by at least a foot, hardly an ideal match or of family resemblance–and there was nothing she wished to add to the speculation spreading across the island like cane fire about the bizarre rampage on campus. So she wrapped her arms around herself and paced the room.

Franck's chest and part of his abdomen were bandaged. He had broken ribs, a concussion, and bruises on his face and arms. He was fortunate. By all accounts, the donkey or bull was about to trample him when some boy armed with a piece of wood charged at the beast, whatever it was, like St. George at the dragon. They–Milton, David, and she–had heard the clanging and screaming and stepped out of the auditorium to see students running in all directions. Milton looked at the crowd and said, "Follow me," as if he knew exactly what was going on. They found Franck under the tree across from the bookshop, surrounded by a group of stunned students. Both the beast and the would-be sticklicker were gone, as if fallen off the edge of the hill.

Marsha didn't know Franck. They had not met during orientation week and hardly noticed each other in the one class they shared with Milton prior to their hike through the gully. He did not exist for her six weeks ago, and if he had been pointed out to her on campus, she would have sworn the course of his life had little or no bearing on her own. Yet her body ached in the places he had been beaten and her head hurt and her thoughts were like wet sand. Marsha kissed her cross. She had never been sick a day in her life–not from a cold, her period, or a fall–now here she was feeling sympathy pains for a stranger and a fear she had not been able to stem since Nana's disappearance.

"That's because you can sense there will be more," Milton announced, entering the room. David was behind him.

"We met on the way up," David said with some impatience.

"How's he doing?" Milton asked.

"Not as sore," Franck whispered from his bed. He hadn't moved, but his eyes were wide open.

Milton stood at the foot of the bed. "I am happy to hear that."

"What happened the other day?" Marsha finally asked.

"It's not what's happened; it's what happe*ning*," he said to her. "It has already begun."

"So–"

"Yes," he said.

"I didn't finish my question," she said.

"That beast *was* a steel donkey."

"I wish you'd stop doing that," David cut in. "There's no need for you to keep reading our thoughts."

Milton stepped toward the window away from David and Marsha, who had gathered on either side of Franck's bed. His eyes glinted grey fire in the sunlight. "Your situation has worsened. There are now *three* beasts afield since the Cataclysm and your... reunion."

"*Three* steel donkeys?" Franck said.

"No. Three different fable beasts. *One* is the steel donkey; the other is a baccou, and the last is the heartless djablès."

"The what?" Franck raised himself on his elbows and felt his sides throb. He was healing fast but still tender.

"Unless the three of you decide to face the Others soon, there will be many more of these beasts. Not just here, but wherever your people are until they have overrun your world."

David, Franck, and Marsha looked at each other then back at Milton without saying a word.

"There are Hunters—I'm merely anticipating your doubts—who are charged with tracking and containing the beasts. The sticklicker may have been one of them. But their numbers are select, and you can't fight on two fronts—you aren't meant to. You have to face the Others if your world is to be saved."

"Saving the world?" Franck scoffed. "Come on, man. Saving the world is something the Americans or the British do—not Caribbean people."

"What does September 11—your 'Cataclysm'—have to do with us?" David asked.

"It's of the world, has happened as a result of the state of the world. The world concerns you no less than it does other peoples."

"Are there any more like us?" said Marsha.

"There should be," said Milton. He felt the presence of the sticklicker on campus only after Franck was attacked. Whatever he was, he now seemed nowhere and everywhere, like a force of Nature Milton could not yet explain.

"So we're it?"

Milton stared at her. "Certain things are going to happen, now. Worse things than the rampage on campus. And where *you* are, these beasts will be."

"Who are these 'Others' you keep talking about? Where do *they* come from?"

Milton sighed. He sat in the chair across from the bed. Marsha thought he looked greyer than the last time they saw each other, which was no more than a week ago. And when she noticed the change in Milton's dusky pallor, David and Franck did, too.

"They are brought by another Elder, my opposite number. It is our duty to bring both sides together for the earth to heal and be whole again."

"What if we don't meet the Others?" said Franck.

"Then more beasts will overrun this island until they've reclaimed the earth."

Franck was about to ask something else when Marsha said, "Does this have anything to do with my grandmother?"

"She was the Guardian who raised you. She was to prepare you for this."

"She's still missing."

Milton did not respond.

"But I'm not yet eighteen," she said.

"Guardian, Elder, Protector, obeah woman–we all have our roles to play. What has happened to the Guardian you call Nana is a mystery. All I know is the three of you are here–"

"Not me," said Franck. He had been shaking his head. "I'm out of this. If what you're saying is all true–*if*–then we have a choice."

"Isn't this the part where we put our hand in the jam gabor, sir?"

Milton smiled at Marsha. He sounded less strident when he answered. "You've already past the test. You three are the Elect, there is no doubt." And to Franck: "And yet, you're right. You have to choose. Each of you. But the decision to fight for your world must be unanimous. The Elect can only act as one."

"If any of us refuses to join the fight...?" asked David without moving his lips.

"Then your world dies."

Marsha was the first to speak aloud again. "That's not much of a choice."

"Much or not"–Milton stood to leave–"it's the one you've got."

19

Mackie sat on a stalagmite, hunched like an exact replica of *The Thinker*. The pose had been his idea, a suggestion to the great Renaissance sculptor, painter, and poet. For some reason, it was like yesterday in his mind, the vineyards full of fragrant fruit, and the sun warm on his back as he drank good wine. The air smelled cleaner then, so much purer humans today would get high. But the waters already started to stink of human waste: filth, refuse, the assassinated or drowned. The fish, always plentiful, were already dying.

"My friend. Lean him this way, and tilt his head so. Yes, just so!"

"Ah! This is not your kind of work, is it? Why not leave the art to artists. Ah! Ah!"

His artist-friend was a man of grunts and growls. He ignored or understood the world best when he worked. Mackie was a Moor at that time. Dark-skinned, at any rate. But his artist-friend took his suggestions of a more ponderous pose for his boy, one that would make men reflect on their true purpose. It worked. For a while.

It only ever seemed to work for a while with humans.

Mackie shifted on the stalagmite rising like a pillar of salt out of the earth. Its tip was smooth as wax and rounded and wide enough to comfortably perch his body's broad backside. Its corresponding column from the ceiling was meters above it, a very insignificant stalactite. Yet Mackie could hear the two calling for each other, to touch.

It would be decades before they did, if they ever did. He heard them moan at his thought. His eyes narrowed; his beard twitched.

"How is the Unbeliever recovering?" he shouted into the darkness to his left.

"Better. And far less 'unbelieving' at the moment."

"Good for him."

"That's good news for all of us, Mackie. None of them is any use dead. The strong one and the flyer are already in agreement."

"What did they ask you?"

"They wanted to know what they are to do while waiting to save the world."

"And what did you tell them?"

"The same as before. 'You live your lives until you are needed.'"

Mackie looked at Milton a moment before bursting with laughter. The crystallized limestone walls shook. His voice boomed through the tunnelled chambers. Stalagmites and stalactites winced.

"They are needed *now*, Milton." Mackie eyed him from a side. Although in human form, too, and susceptible to human actions, he abhorred pretence. "You didn't tell them their time is almost up, then?"

"In so many words, no."

"Godblimuh. You didn't tell them *every*thing?"

"They are aware of what they need to know."

"For now."

Mackie hopped off his pedestal. Milton approached him. He dropped his voice. "It's too soon to tell them everything, man. This is a different age–"

"They are no different from past humans," Mackie flared, brushing Milton aside. "They are not likely to follow."

"You mean *lead*."

Silence.

"Many of their people live a hundred years or more, Mackie–"

"We agree they are strong, but you didn't tell them about their sacrifice?"

"Not as such," Milton said, adding: "Nor about the solstice."

"We have a deadline, Milton. They do not have all year."

"That much they do know," he said. "But these humans can't be coerced. You know that as well as I."

"The steel donkey and the baccou appeared within days of each other. Fast, fast, even by our timepieces, one then the next. Look here," he said, twirling into the air, arms outstretched. "Look around Harrison's Cave, at the shapes of its inhabitants. This whole underground, with its formations and manifestations, is a wonder. They call this centuries-old chamber the Cathedral. Listen, Milton. Listen to the sound of its supplicants."

Milton heard a hushed hissing, the drip, drip of trickling water, and the creaking made by shifting rock. From inside the rock, he heard the cries of trapped souls–duppies, Mackie now called them– seeking release, the spirits of slaves, seamen, midwives, and other captives, striving to be free again. He saw them pulsing like a bright, hot heartbeat just beneath the smooth sediment, the Known and Unknown Worlds mixing to make the benign malevolent.

The coral had started to come alive again, and with it these beasts.

"They may not be next, or half as destructive as the steel donkey or baccou, but in time they will gather enough force to gain release, like a wave rushing out of a shell."

"I have told the Elect the truth. That their people's only hope lies in them."

"Then you've told them nothing they don't already know."

"All three of them must be in agreement. Their decision to sacrifice themselves must be unanimous and selfless. They understand this."

Mackie was doubtful. "We're running out of time, man. Or is it you're running short on faith?"

"They are like lambs, Mackie, not warriors."

"Then lead them to my righteous slaughter." Mackie's hazel eyes crackled. His hair spiked in peaks around his head. "Your charges *will* fight. I will see to that."

Milton said nothing. Then: "They will fight, Machiavelli."

Mackie thought a moment. "Yes, they will. And they will lose. And *you* will see to that."

After a while, "I have a class to teach," Milton said. "I have to prepare."

Mackie nodded. He could feel the dawn. It was time to move back into the light.

20

"'Later stories penned while away from my native Barbados are, I find, calmer and quieter in tone. Their setting is the realm of youth, from which few of us escape without some sentimentality for the people we knew or the places we often frequented; never thinking that, one day, we would no longer visit them....'" Milton paused. He did not sound like himself. He did not *not* sound like himself, but he didn't sound like himself, either. He sounded like two people at once, like himself and quite possibly the author of the words he was reading, urbane and Bajan, measured and quietly confident. Yet he never said he knew Jimmy Weatherhead or seemed to be assuming the voice of a gentle giant. He merely spoke, and the "other" was there, sometimes above his voice, sometimes beneath it. Milton glanced back down at the page. "'The stories I would vouch for are "Lean Streets," "Chance Encounter," "Neither Here Nor Home," and "If Memory Serves." These four have proven most enduring, for what they gave me in writing and still offer in reading.'"

Milton looked up. "The author. January 1993." He closed the book he was reading from and tucked it in one of the large, embroidered pockets of his shirtjac. "Four out of four*teen.*" He began to work the room.

"Here is our starting point. Simply because an author recommends a selection of his own work is no indication of its worth." Milton looked up again. "It is possible to love cow dung."

The class chuckled uneasily.

"But Weatherhead was a Caribbean man who understood self praise was no praise. No, he was on to something–as *Revelations*, the title of his last collection of short stories, suggests. There was a quality, a complexity, and a depth to the quartet of stories he singles out that went beyond those of others he had written, and certainly those imagined by his contemporaries at the time. You've all read them?"

The question, rather a statement, was rhetorical. Milton, from Class One, had impressed himself upon the students as a professor whose assignments and readings could not wait, whether his class was a core course or an elective. It wasn't what he said to you if you hadn't done the readings; it was how he stared at you: making you feel low and criminal.

Besides, "Lean Streets" and the three highlighted stories were the only fiction by Weatherhead they were studying. The other work by Weatherhead the class was promised was "Imprimatur," an essay that appeared in his newspaper column days before his death, and a transcript of his last radio interview with a Canadian journalist who later wrote a slim, unauthorized biography of the author.

Milton opened his arms to the class with a smile. "Weatherhead points us to these four stories. There must be a reason, beyond personal pleasure... or pride."

A hand tentatively went up. A young woman with a tam over short locks. Thin face and big eyes made bigger by nervousness.

"Yes, Miss Jones." Another thing about the professor that surprised them: he knew all their names—first, last, and evidently middle. They were seventy-two students—a sizeable survey class. None of them had ever experienced such lack of anonymity and didn't know how this total recall was possible for a man who met with them for three hours once a week.

"I've read them all, sir—" She coughed to speak more clearly in the frigid auditorium—"I mean, the four you assigned, and the others in the collection, and I like them, but there was something about these four that was... different?"

"Or do you mean 'disturbing'?"

"Yes! That's it." Miss Jones sounded relieved.

"How?"

The girl started then stopped. "I'm not sure. I mean, in tone, maybe. In their urgency–or ugliness. Of people." She strained to be coherent. Tried not to cover her eyes or mouth.

"Of Caribbean people. Of the Caribbean."

"Yes," she said with a jolt. Then Miss Jones shrugged, at a loss. "I guess so. In 'Lean Streets,' people are compared to animals, or animals to people, and time and religion are not the salvation you would expect them to be for the main character, a poor Trini gal."

The class chuckled, a little more at ease this time.

Gaining courage, Miss Jones said: "It's as if she's living in heaven and hell–on earth–but doesn't know it, or how to escape it...."

Milton smiled at the thin, big-eyed girl with new locks on her head. "It sometimes feels that way, doesn't it?"

The class stopped laughing. Miss Jones had nothing else to say.

"You may have a point, Miss Jones. One last question: Why is this book of stories called *Revelations*? I know Weatherhead tells us; we have his explanation in his Author's Note." Milton plucked the book from his pocket. "But what are we meant to see revealed?"

A few brave hands went up. Milton waved them down. "Not so fast, not so fast," he said. "You'll have the whole semester to mess up that one."

Milton watched the students leave one by one. David was absent, Marsha, too. He was tempted to ask their classmates for news of them but decided against the tactic. Franck was to be released from hospital that afternoon. It was possible they went to be with him when he got out.

Better to be certain.

Milton closed the doors with a sweep of his hands and opened his thoughts: first to the campus, then to the city, its surrounding villages and communities, then to the entire parish, until he could feel the Elect and, like an undercurrent, the growing presence of other forces in Nature.

21

She took the stairs to the ward four steps at a time. She would have leapt from landing to landing if not for the traffic on them. The chain and cross around her neck bounced with each bound. She was dressed in matching magenta athletic gear, but who'd believe her performance was the result of too much Ovaltine tea or an overachieving school sports programme? She wasn't winded and never broke a sweat, no matter the exertion. As long as she had known herself, she had always enough strength—never more or less—to pull, push, or jump whatever she wanted. Rounding the corner toward Franck's room, Marsha pictured Franck running at the speed of light and David flying unaided through outer space.

Hospitals in the Caribbean, like hospitals in the movies, all looked the same to Marsha: as dingy as their Hollywood counter-parts were scoured, as open-air as those onscreen were shut-off. In reality, this one wasn't so bad. An antiseptic scent bleached every hallway and room, and funding, staffing, and expansion prob-lems meant Barbados' only public hospital was where most of the nation's babies were safely delivered, where most of the surgeries were successfully performed, and where accidents and emergencies were referred to when private doctors had done their best.

Franck was packing when she knocked at his door.

"What are you doing here?" he said.

Marsha crossed her arms with a slight smile.

"Now is that any way to talk to your sister Elect?"

"Sorry," he said, going back to his packing. "I thought you and David would be in class. With Milton."

"We *should* be," she said. "But I thought you'd need a ride home, and David had to meet his girlfriend—did you know he had a girlfriend?"

"Sashanna," Franck nodded.

"Sashanna. (Of course you'd know; you're guys.) At Sam Lord's Castle for some auction. He tells me she's really into all that Bygone Barbados stuff."

"Yeah."

Marsha moved from the doorway. Frank zipped his bag.

"So how are you feeling?" she said.

"The doctors say I'm well enough to go."

"That's not what I asked."

"I know. I just don't know what to expect when I get out of here."

"None of us does. We never know what's in the next pasture... or what might fall from the sky."

"Yeah, but before it was only Mr. Callender's black belly sheep or Miss Mavis' coconuts. We didn't have to check for steel donkeys."

"Or little pink men with big rockstones," she said.

He laughed. She sat in the chair across from the bed. It faced the window overlooking Constitution River; she had a view straight into Bridgetown. The spire of the Parliament Buildings' clock tower was visible from here, draped with a limp Broken Trident. An extreme long shot. What was showing at The Globe drive-in tonight? It couldn't be better than what she and the others were playing in. Whenever Nana could, she took Marsha to the movies. Sometimes as a reward, sometimes as a distraction, depending on what Marsha had gotten up to. Her smile vanished.

"Nana's still missing."

"I'm sorry," he said.

"She's not online; she's not answering her cell. I used to hear from that woman every day, no matter what. It's like she always knew where and when to find me. Do you know what that's like, talking to someone you love every single day of your life?"

Franck shook his head. "No."

"Now, I can't hear Nana at all, at all." Marsha thought a moment before saying what she did next: "Do you think they, Milton and this other he mentioned... Mackie, really are angels but don't want us to know? Maybe they can't, like Nicolas Cage with Meg Ryan in *City of Angels*."

"They could be something *close* to angels. I really don't know."

"If they were," Marsha said, staring into the sunlight streaming through the window without blinking, "they wouldn't be the cause of all this, would they? God wouldn't be." She rubbed her cross between two fingers as she spoke.

"It depends on what you believe. This wouldn't be the first reported fight between heaven and hell involving a Milton," Franck said.

Marsha ignored the allusion. "Do you believe him?"

Franck slumped on the bed. There were certain thoughts he, too, must have been avoiding. "Part of me wants to, because it would explain so much about my life. But then I think, 'Barbadians–responsible for saving the world?' I just don't see it."

"But why not? Where is Barbados? Isn't Barbados part of the world? Everything that happens in the rest of the world seems to affect us at some point."

"And how often does what we do affect the rest of the world?"

Marsha was silent.

"How *well* do you know Montreal?" she asked.

"I grew up there."

"So you know the city."

"I know LaSalle–that's where we lived–and parts of downtown."

"Nana lives in LaSalle."

Silence again.

"If what Milton said *is* true, then your grandmother... she'll soon be like mine and David's... Guardians."

"But if what he's saying *is* true, then she shouldn't be gone–not yet. I have to find her. If she's still alive, I have to."

"You know she could be anywhere–"

"Or nowhere. Wouldn't you want to know if it were your Aunt or Uncle? I hear you; Milton says we're supposed to be here. What if *this* is what I'm meant to do?"

Franck stared at her. He was born in Barbados but raised in Canada. He never felt at home there, and his Aunt and Uncle, despite speaking impeccable French, Greek, Latin, and Italian, were to him the oddest fit in Quebec society. Their lives always seemed unsettled, as if they were watching and waiting for something to happen that they couldn't be sure would. And it took all their energy, so turned their house into a dread place he felt uncomfortable inviting friends no matter how often his Aunt or Uncle told him he could. They watched and died waiting. It wasn't until the attack of the steel donkey that it occurred to Franck who they might have been watching, or what they were waiting for.

"Hey," Marsha called out softly to him. "What do you say? You up to helping out this lil Trini gal?"

Frank laughed. "You're far from little or helpless. Aren't you? But you may be right–you are right. If it were *my* Aunt or Uncle, I'd want to know what happened to them. I've had enough of Milton the Mad... and whatever the rest of this is about. When do you want to leave?"

Marsha held up a credit card. "When's the next flight to Montreal?" She smiled at the expression on his face. It was truly priceless. "Is only one uh we to pack, eh?"

"You got a winter coat?" he replied. "It's fall in Montreal."

"I don't need one–but I've got something I can wear."

"OK," he said.

"Leh we go," she said.

"You're where, again? Off to where?"

David stood outside the gates to Sam Lord's Castle, talking to Franck on his cell. He was late for the auction and had been hurrying to meet Sashanna when it rang.

"We're at the airport. The plane leaves in about an hour. We can't afford to be out longer than a week. Marsha's putting all of this on her card, and then there's school—"

David wished them good luck. He was less surprised than he sounded. He agreed with Franck: Marsha's Nana might have some answers for them all, if any of what Milton told them was true; if she was still alive. Almost nothing of Theophilus or Huldah was left after they died. What little there was, he had to hold fast before it was scattered like pitched marbles. The house and forge were sold by lawyers on retainer; David could only guess at his parents' ages for the headstones—there were no records of their births either at the parish church or the Bridgetown registry. When he dreamt them now, they appeared to him in parts, never whole: a patch of dark skin or white hair streaked red, a massive fist or bent back. Even their voice and touch had faded from his memory.

David wanted to tell Franck and Marsha, "Don't worry about anything here," but he couldn't say how Milton would take their leaving.

"How will you find her if she's not at the apartment?"

"If she's missing," Franck said, "we'll go to the police. They may already be looking for her."

"Walk good," David said.

"You, too."

22

On the other side of Bridgetown, toward the west, three witches rocked. Floorboards crick-cracked like cane trash, their chairs swung mad as cow bells keeping time.

"He has her!" said Black Cat.

"How?" asked Sly Mongoose.

"Who knows?" declared Green Monkey.

"The baccra with two hearts!" They chanted.

They stopped rocking with a thud.

"As with Londinium and Gotham, the blood of the Diaspora is strong in Ville-Marie."

"… the place of the royal mountain is in ascent."

"Ville-Marie is the old name for an ancient place."

"Still part of Our World, the New World."

"He was *never* meant to be there."

"The Elect have sent to find him."

"Gone to find *her*, you mean."

"The fast one's Guardians were there first."

"And died."

"Their duty."

"Died with them."

"Did it, then?"

They began to rock again, slowly, slowly.

"The situation is worse."

"Than we feared."

"We should have been more vigilant."

"We should have *known*."

Black Cat: "We *did* know."

"Know what?"

"Great lizards were *thought* before they appeared."

"Two by two. Two by two."

"No ark could save them."

Sly Mongoose: "What do we do?"

Black Cat: "Nothing."

Green Monkey: "Yet."

Together: "As earth follows sun, and moon follows earth, child follows mother. Earth, sun, and moon. Yes, yes."

23

Sam Lord's Castle had sunk into disrepair since the days when Sashanna visited on excursion in secondary school. The old regency mansion, a centrepiece of the resort chain that owned it, was still a heritage building, and its name (if little else about the estate these days) in the minds of Barbadians and rich visitors was second only to Sandy Lane on the wealthy west coast. But looka wha white people would covet, doh, Sashanna marvelled to herself, strolling the halls.

She laughed out loud.

Not just white people. Sashanna adored the castle's mahogany columns and plastered ceilings. She wanted to spend the night in Lord's own four-poster beds or hang a ball dress in one of the wardrobes in which he probably stashed stolen treasure and his best rum. Sam Lord's Castle was the only castle Sashanna had ever visited in her life. Because it was said to be one, built over three years starting in 1820, and stood as one, gleaming white and domineering, every time she returned to study its artefacts she felt like a princess from over and away in Africa. Sam Lord's Castle was where Sashanna first learned to admire and then appreciate the works of the past for what, long after their creation, they tell about a people–her people, but it could be any people.

But the castle's age was showing in its sun-bleached bones: peeling paint, rusty latches, salt-pitted hardwood, and cobwebbed rafters–it was barely clinging to its three-star status. This was not the first time the castle had been allowed to crumble... if "allowed" was the right word, Sashanna reflected as she followed the signs to the auction. The salt air at Long Bay could eat out your heart. Barbados would have swallowed the poor Englishman's palace by now if others didn't keep coming to its rescue. Sashanna had heard on one of the radio call-in programmes that its present owners were interested in selling the property. It was in the red. Since the days of Sam Lord, it probably always had been.

Sam Lord, "The Regency Rascal," was a dry-land pirate. Or so they—whoever tells stories and passes them on—say. Each corner of the castle, almost diabolically, faced a cardinal point. Lord used to lure ships with bright lights onto the rocks at Long Bay, then thief their cargo. And still he died a pauper, in debt.

Sashanna turned a corner and entered a large, empty room. The signs ended here, and she worried David would miss her. She saw a clear-skinned man in grey jacket and blue bowtie by a closed door at the other end of the room. She heard noises from the adjoining room, like people liming, and loud classical music played above the steady voice of an auctioneer.

"Hello," she said. "Excuse me." But without turning the man opened the door to the adjoining room and closed it behind him.

Sashanna steupsed her teeth. She was sure the man heard her. She opened the door and entered the room.

And the room was empty. The man wasn't there, and there was another door at the end of the room. Then foreign voices swelled from the other side of that closed door, *verstossen, verlassen, zertrüm-mert ewig alle der Natur,* and the music surged, like a wolf gang come to swallow her, or mad Queen of the Band, and there were the crashing sounds of laughter, bells, and glass breaking.

Sashanna knocked at the other door. "Hello? Hello?" The scar on her cheek itched. The room became warm and wet, and sweat dripped from her back and armpits.

"Are you looking for me?"

She spun around. It was not the clear-skinned man in the jacket and tie but an old white man in a worn velvety brown frock coat with a scarlet scarf loosely knotted around his neck. The puffed cuffs of his white silk shirt were ragged. He was an Englishman–he sounded like an Englishman–but Sashanna was confused by his clothes, and now the noise from the other room didn't sound like a lime at all but a drunken ball where men and women were being bought and sold for a song. The Englishman smelled of iron and salt.

"Are you looking for me?" he said again.

"No–de auction. Uh just lost–"

He advanced, and she retreated, pressing against the door.

He repeated his question.

Sashanna didn't understand why he kept asking her the same thing over and over, or how every time he spoke the words they sounded different; they had a new inflection or emphasis, yet without any clearer meaning to her.

She stared at his ruddy cheeks and chin, his white watery eyes; he was familiar, though she was just as certain she didn't know the madman. When he raised his hands, he held a lighthouse keeper's lantern on a chain in one and an ivory-handle dagger in the other. The lamp glowed mossy yellow.

Sashanna couldn't get around him, but she knew she couldn't go through the door he was trying to push her through. Something about the noise from the other side was terrifying and unnatural–just like the man.

Her eyes widened. He lashed Sashanna across her scarred cheek with the light of the lamp. Her scar burned where the light touched her and she dropped, flesh seared. The Englishman held the dagger above his head.

He spat the sinister phrase one more time.

"She isn't," said a voice from above him. "But I am."

The Englishman snorted a smile at Milton. He charged him, swinging his lantern, its yellow light slicing like a sword.

Milton caught the creature by the neck with one hand, stopping the lantern in mid-motion.

"Back. Back. It is not yet your time."

"Soon," said the creature, dissipating, "it will be all our time."

The lantern and dagger clanged on the floor. The noises from the other room stopped. Sashanna was barely conscious.

Milton lifted her and carried her out.

David intercepted them in the hallway. "Sashanna!" He flew to her when he saw her in Milton's arms. "What happened? We were supposed to meet in the foyer for an auction. What are you doing here?"

"She was led astray by a duppy. Sam Lord himself."

"What?"

"She'll be fine–only a little bruised–but you are the lucky one. He would have killed her, or worse, for his pleasure."

Milton rested Sashanna on a double-ended mahogany couch.

"He was looking for me?" said David. "This is my fault, then?"

Milton's eyes crackled like kindling. "He wasn't looking *for* you; he was prowling because he sensed there was *only* you."

David was silent.

"Where are they?" Milton said. "Franck and Marsha."

"They've left." David briefly debated lying to the Elder before remembering, just as quickly, how easily Milton had found him. "They're on their way to Montreal."

"To search for Marsha's grandmother."

David nodded. "But how is it you knew I was here, but you don't know where they are?"

"Wherever you are, whatever you do, I can see you–once you are on this island. The further away you are from this rock, the weaker our connection. If the other two are in Canada, they are as much on their own as we are."

David looked up from Sashanna. "They'll only be gone a few days–"

"Which is time none of us can afford."

"They're trying to find Marsha's *grand*mother."

"*If* she's alive," Milton said. He pointed to Sashanna. "Have I *not* made myself clear to the three of you? The *long*er it takes for you to decide to act as one, the *worse* Barbados and then the rest of your world becomes with beasts like Sam Lord's duppy."

Milton reached into the left breast pocket of his shirtjac. "When she wakes, give her this." He handed David a small, leather flask tied at its opening with fine silver twine. "Sprinkle some on her lips. Then take her far away from here and turn all the clothes she's wearing inside out, to keep the duppy from returning."

"What's this?" David asked. The contents of the flask felt grainy in his hands through the leather's thin skin, like guinea corn meal.

"Herbs. You would call it a potion, but there's little to no magic in it. It will ease her pain. And her memory."

Milton turned and began to walk away, as casually as he had rounded the hall with Sashanna.

David called after him. "What are you going to do?"

He answered without looking back. "To tell Mackie what has happened. What else?"

24

In Daren's house, there was a room no one except himself ever entered. Even he had hoped to be in it infrequently during his lifetime. In the last two months, he had spent some part of every day or night in it, sharpening tools, readying weapons, tracking prey. His wife knew what was in the room—Nina was not offset by the glass bottles big enough to fit a little child, the mortars and pestles, by the latest combat armour or rifle-fired nets, the antique maps or compasses, whenever she looked in, and that was almost never. A few times she saw Daren, near exhausted, come and go, closing the door softly behind him so not to disturb her or the baby. She knew what he was doing in there. He loved her, and he told her, and she believed in him. She knew what he was and what he had inherited, and the danger of them both. But she never stepped into the room, whether he was there or not, and Daren thought he understood why.

Daren traced his fingers along a map of Graeme Hall Swamp. It was lately being rehabilitated into a Nature sanctuary. The change in name, which was still misleading, meant nothing. Its nomenclature suggested Barbadians of different eras understood the space. They did not. The same green herons that had been migrating there since his ancestors' time in the island still came and went. The red mangrove was still among the most resilient in the region. The woods and water acted as a barrier between the noisy world of men and a quieter world of sandpiper and white land crab, muffling sound, concealing movement. It was the perfect place for the beast to hide after scurrying from the gullies and tumbling from the trees.

The map Daren reviewed was a hunting map, circa 1969. The person who sold it to him said it was used by the island's first prime minister, who kept a cabin in the swamp and went there with his political cronies and sometimes with friends to shoot birds and smoke Cuban cigars, or to get away from women, wife, and family for a while. The former prime minister's map, personally charted by him, a World War II army vet, showed all the known paths into the swamp to this day, and a few that appeared on none of the plans presented to Town & Country by the designers of the "sanctuary" as a tourist attraction. Daren was reminded, as he folded the map and placed it in the satchel on his left hip, that it was futile to order Nature, delusional for humans to think they could condition it.

There was no sign of the steel donkey. Daren thought it could be hiding in the caves, maybe in St. Lucy. It was possible given its first fight that that beast was not his responsibility. He couldn't say for certain. He had felt the presence of a third beast on the island briefly. There then gone.

All his dreams were now waking ones. In the last, he was close. To what, though? There were many eyes watching him beneath a moonless night sky. He felt afraid as they grew larger than spotlights, brighter than stars. They blinded him, and his world faded to white. After that, he felt nothing.

Daren intended to make this his final encounter with the baccou. He didn't want to disturb Nina or Corrie any more than he already had. He would be gone only a few days.

25

Mackie sat in the centre of De Gateway Café, watching people come and go. It was karaoke night. Someone was trying to sing to a laconic, syncopated, heartbreak-beat Barbadians claimed as spouge. To this breathless jig, Mackie preferred the unruly military march of tuk–the peal of the pennywhistle, the dance of the drum– or even the driving revolutions of calypso with its strange dancehall and baptist hybrids. November was the season of Independence in Barbados. It was only October; someone was starting the celebrations early. The indigenous rhythm was a favourite of the season. Mackie would have thought Independence was something celebrated every day, not once a year, but this was how humans honoured their achievements: in showy, stagy, sing-along bursts. Mackie closed his eyes, opened them a moment later. He gulped his beer, asking himself if this songbird named Robin he anticipated would validate any of the organized noise Bajans created as music.

Someone shouted for the singer to stop and the television to be turned up. The President of the United States was giving a press conference. The Americans had just invaded Afghanistan. A holy war on terror and its abettors had begun.

Humanity had slipped fast since the occurrence of the Cataclysm. Arabs, and East Indians who resembled Arabs to myopic Western-trained eyes, were now suspect at borders. Civil liberties countries had taken in some cases centuries to institute were being curtailed, encroached upon, in a number of instances utterly suspended, legally and illegally, in pursuit of the enemy. Air travel for business or pleasure would never be as leisurely as it once was. Men, women, and children were being asked by customs officers to remove more than their hats and jackets. Anything that was a weapon or could conceal a weapon was banned. So, Mackie thought, pocket knives aboard commercial flights have finally been restricted. But a group of determined men and women with loose thread in their shirts or ballpoint pens could still cause enough confusion. That their objectives were harder to achieve would only make their sacrifice more glorious. All it ever took was the skill and the will to hurt others, and not even so much of the first in the end.

There were limits to the restrictions any of these countries could place on each other for the protection of their people. The television was on, and the Barbadians in De Gateway Café were afraid. Getting a visa for America was already a humiliating process for many of them. The embassy wanted a certain class of traveller, people who were not too dark or too alien or who would not under any condition seek to stay longer than permitted. Their government had started to treat the rest of the world (and many of its own) as suspect, criminal, long before. Individual thoughts melded into a frenetic buzz. The Barbadians in De Gateway Café did not know about the release of the beasts across their island, but they knew they, too, were not safe at 30,000 feet. What was their Prime Minister going to do to protect them? What could he do?

Heh. How *would* humanity regain its footing? Mackie gulped his Banks, swept a cool hand over his bushy face, and belched heartily. He knew. But they would never believe it, most certainly not nations like America or Britain right now. Grenada had enough medicinal herbs, roots, and bark to remedy half the world's ailing, yet neither the Americans nor the British would ever accept that. Nor, for that matter, would Grenadians. Fortunately for the rest of humanity, it wasn't their conviction that counted, this time. *If* humanity would indeed be fortunate.

De Gateway Café was Milton's hangout. Not his, but it was good for a shot of rum or cold beer, which Mackie increasingly preferred, often with an order of Sam's herb-stuffed fried chicken and chips. Elders like him and Milton were human (more or less) only once every fifty or sixty or seventy years, and never in the same form twice. Time faded experience for all in existence. He was starting to remember why humans clung to life as they did. Mackie appreciated what he was and had never desired to be anything other, but, Godblimuh, he enjoyed the physicality of his humanity, what his five senses added to his other perceptions, and filling a body to bursting with spirit. Being human was a way, for him, of exceeding *his* limitations. And for Milton, too, though Mackie knew his comrade would never put it that way.

"No. I wouldn't."

Mackie didn't turn around. "You see how well I know you?"

"What are you doing here?"

"It is also easier in this form to shut out the roar and whining of the universe. Some of the time, at least," said Mackie. "Why are *you* here?"

Milton stood before him. "Two of the Elect are out of the island."

"What? You lie."

"Franck and Marsha–"

"You know their names mean nothing to me–"

"–the fast one and the strong one–gone to Canada to find the girl's grandmother, who has apparently disappeared."

"Not possible."

Milton shook his head. He sat and signalled Sam for what had become his usual, a malt. She gave Milton a look that told him she was upset, though not with him. She and Cooper weren't agreeing. A fight–predictably enough–but this time about Johnny. Nobody had seen him since the start of the Cataclysm. He usually came and went at even intervals. Sam was worried about him. Johnny had gone missing, just like her brother. Cooper wished she cared as much about where he slept as she did about some parro artist who couldn't afford the food she gave him, much less to buy her a meal, or a vagabond *half*-brother who would find her fast enough soon as he needed money. At least, Sam said, she cared bout somebody other than sheself.

"I felt something was wrong, but I had no idea...," said Mackie, unconcerned by the memories Milton was tapping.

"Nor I," said Milton, his thoughts returning to the present.

Mackie gave his comrade a hard look. "Most people don't want the truth, Milton. They want a coddling lie. The Elect ain't even see a star pitch yet. But the truth is if these three young men and women fight for their world, they will not return to it."

"They know this, Machiavelli."

"And they ran."

"Only two of them. To save a dear old lady."

Mackie finished his beer in one long swallow. "*My* charges wait on The Other Side. They must meet in the middle with yours. We can't change the rules for a band of force-ripe, own-way, hard-ears upstarts." Mackie stood. "Take your malt–or leave it–it's time to see the three obeah women down the gap."

Mackie dashed some coins onto the table, and they multiplied to cover their exact bill. Milton got up.

"For once," he said, "I won't argue with you."

26

Mackie and Milton walked across the car park shaded by casuarinas to the road that led into it. Three houses down on the right was the obeah women's dwelling, ringed with three herb gardens. It was a moonless night, starless, too; the absence of warmth and light would have troubled them had they been susceptible to such discomforts.

Milton knocked on the chattel house's thin double doors. A key rattled. The doors swung out and they stepped in. Oil lamps lit the vestibule, which smelt of circe-bush.

Two of the obeah women stood before them in the half-darkness of the front room, blocking their path. They said nothing, simply stared at the Elders, neither distressed nor surprised by their visit.

"Good evening–" Mackie began.

"It can't be so good if the two of you are here," said Black Cat, bursting through her sisters' guard with her walking stick levelled at him.

"'Today is a funny night,'" said Milton, quoting the old Bajan proverb.

"But none as funny as this," hissed Black Cat.

"Not quite," conceded Milton.

"We've come to see you," said Mackie, cutting in, "because–"

"Me? Come to see *me?*" Black Cat screeched. Sly Mongoose and Green Monkey stood on either side of her. The three obeah women were perched on their sticks, their lips pushed up like beaks.

"We have no time for this," bellowed Mackie, his eyes crackling.

"No time for *man*ners? In *our* house?" The obeah women's sticks began to rise.

Milton waved them down. "You are right," he said. "But so is this Elder. We *need* your insight."

Their sticks remained cocked. Black Cat spoke. "It is not allowed," she said.

Calmly Milton eyed her, took note of the length of her yellowing nut-brown hair, the seagreen that still coloured her eyes. "No more so than it is for an obeah woman to have been handsome, once?"

Black Cat cut her eyes at Milton. For a moment–one improbable moment–her features were familiar to him. "I'm beyond all that," she said to him.

"Then you should know that two of the Elect are missing."

"Yes." The obeah women lowered their sticks. Answered in unison: "We know."

Milton looked at Mackie then back at the witches. Even though they had said it, the two Elders could not believe it.

"And you did *nothing*–to alert us?" cried Mackie.

"It is not *our* job to do–or say. Ours is to *see*. Our vision is clear. As is our conscience."

Mackie bristled. "This is bad for all of us," he warned Black Cat. "For this world and those like us now a part of it. We need your help, not back talk."

"That is not allowed," repeated Black Cat. "But we can *try*."

The heads of the three obeah women tilted toward each other. The room filled with the sound of chatter, like a gaggle of blackbirds.

"Where is the Guardian of the one christened Marsha?" said Milton.

"Gone," the three obeah women whispered above the twitter.

"Something we don't know," said Mackie. "Guardians don't disappear. They *die*. All things die. Almost."

Another loud whisper: "But *never* before their time. This one was taken, then."

"By whom?" said Milton.

"... A hellraiser... a heartbreaker...."

"Riddles, riddles," Mackie muttered to himself. He hated obeah women for their ease with them and mistrusted mystic visions—far more reliable to circumvent time and space—and he could tell Milton was also growing annoyed... but they all had their part to play. "What can we do?" he said.

"What you didn't fail to do before." The birds stopped, swallowed by Black Cat. She turned to Mackie with an arid smile. "Is *that* clear enough for you?"

Milton shoved Mackie, who was cussing the three obeah women, out the door. In another instant, the sparks in his eyes would have ignited, and they would have retaliated with whatever spell they had been brewing, and they all may as well have lit a beacon for the beasts to find them, or put up a billboard announcing to Barbadians their existence. It wasn't the obeah women's fault—or Milton's comrade's—that he had lost track of two of the Elect. It was no one else's, finally, but his own.

27

Franck came out of the washroom and zipped up his jacket. "Ready," he said to Marsha, who was hunched over their table.

"Gimme a moment, eh?" she said, stabbing a forkful of sauce-covered French fries clumped with cheese curd.

Franck shook his head. "How can your quasi-Trini palate stomach that stuff?"

Marsha held the white Styrofoam bowl to her mouth, drained the remainder of its contents then dabbed her lips with a paper napkin. "Cheese, chips, gravy. Some of the best foods are your poutine."

He sucked his teeth.

"What? It was on *all* the sites I visited–*feted* as if it were Quebecois ambrosia. And you've never tried it?"

"Nah."

"You're such a staid speedster."

Outside the pizzeria, by the greenwood gazebo, Franck checked his watch again. "I told him we'd be there by 11. It's 10:47. You sure you can keep up with me? We have enough time to take the 110. I won't run too fast but–"

"I'm sure." Marsha raised her hood. She was dressed in a black-and-red track suit. "Athletics was my thing at secondary school. As was kickboxing and bodybuilding and football and netball.... I'm faster than the fastest woman alive, though a tad slower than you, it seems. There's no way I could outrun you, if I had to, but I'm sure I can match your jog."

"Then let's go."

They started up the bicycle path stretching along the St. Lawrence River into Lachine. It was cold, and only a few seniors out for a smoke or walking their dogs trailed this part of LaSalle Boulevard.

Once navigated during the French colony's rich fur trade, the large river moved with an icy slowness, its leaden colours mirroring the cloud-clogged sky. Oaks and poplars and maples lined the shore like guards, stripped by the season.

Franck glanced to his right. They passed the white brick duplex where he grew up, near the Anglican church on 75th Avenue. He did not think, after his Aunt's and Uncle's deaths in April, that he'd be back so soon. The duplex was sold by a relative of theirs he never knew existed until days before the funeral. The money was then put in trust, for him to go back to Barbados and continue his studies. He thought the last part of that plan had always been his. Franck had no intention to return to Canada. Ever. Six months later, he really hadn't missed Montreal, except for his Aunt and Uncle. The doctors said they died minutes apart, simply of old age. He was surprised to discover he didn't know their exact birthdates and had to guess at them for the headstones. David said he had to do the same for his parents–or Guardians, as Milton called them, men and women who were far more than their keepers or trainers.

Apart from finding her grandmother, the first thing Marsha wanted to do upon landing at Dorval was try a poutine and ride the metro into the "underground city." She had never visited her grandmother in Montreal but read it had one of the largest West Indian communities in the world outside of the Caribbean, and still ranked high after New York, London, and Toronto. Most English-speaking immigrants had come in the 50's or 60's, after World War II and regional independence freed up movement and opportunities, though Franck never knew when his Aunt or Uncle made the journey. Not that any of this told Marsha or him why Nana decided one morning in May to leave the house she'd owned for years in Tobago, her kitchen garden and evening sea baths, her Saturday morning cricket and coconut water, for a one-and-a-half in a cramped city suburb. He was preparing to leave the country as she was arriving. He could no longer laugh off with friends the mock Jamaican accents on all the Caribbean characters on TV, or questions about "steel drums" by grinning white Quebecois girls at parties, or teachers referring to Guyana as "Guiana" and Barbados as "The Barbadoes," even when corrected. And he never had the slightest inclination to explain to well-meaning teachers in primary school how he felt when a student called him *nègre* and they asked him about it afterward, in the hallway–taking *him* out of the classroom as if *he* had done something wrong. "How are you? *Triste? Faché? Il ne faut pas avoir honte....*" Why the France would he feel ashamed? Yet Franck also knew the carnival culture his people projected never helped: many viewed the region as not a real place, with real people or real problems, which was what it was to him: Back Home, that's all. Outside of their rum, beaches, and Jamaica, did anyone know or care about their philosophies, revolutions, sciences, or writers like James Weatherhead?

In covering the distance on foot, Franck realized he really hadn't lived far from the detective's house. The police officer at the station across from the pizzeria, Sergeant Delvecchio, was surprisingly helpful. People went missing every day in the greater Montreal area, he said, and without further evidence of a crime, it would take him weeks to look into it. But he knew a man–*antillais,* like them; a member of their *communauté*–who specialized in this area. He had assisted the police before–the sergeant knew him personally and recommended him highly. "I've never worked with a young private investigator with such... *c'est quoi le mot juste?...* insight? He may," said the sergeant, searching his desk drawer for one of the detective's cards, "already be familiar with certain *éléments* of your case."

Franck pulled up. Marsha wasn't doubled over when they reached McDuff's house, but she was visibly winded.

"You all right?" he said.

She nodded, breathing deeply. "I'm not accustomed... to... catchin muh breath...."

"I wasn't running fast–"

"I know–you weren't–"

"You were keeping up."

"I was... but... *boy,* lemma tell yuh... your *slow* is some *fast.* I've *never* felt this way after running with someone."

Franck smiled a little. "You mean, you've never competed on a level playing field before."

Marsha stared at him–not in an unkind way, but not in as friendly a way as a local passerby might have thought. She had never doubted her abilities–they were, to her, natural, no unfair advantage–until now, running against him, *not* with him. Gradually, she smiled back at Franck. "I guess I haven't. Have you?"

"Never."

"How do you think the others are coping, then?"

"I'd think about the same as us," he said.

"No more steel donkeys?"

Franck didn't answer.

"You still aren't convinced," she said.

"Are you? Why are we here if you think we should be Back Home?"

"Because of Nana; she's my only reason. Why are *you* here?"

He dropped the issue. "Shall we knock?"

"Yes," she said, straightening. "Let's shall."

Julius C. McDuff answered and hurried them into his den. His receptionist was out; his shirtsleeves were rolled, and his home office was very quiet. His eyes were drawn, as if he had been up all night.

"Please," he said, motioning to the armchairs before his desk, and both Franck and Marsha sat.

28

In their first meeting, McDuff was abrupt at times but never rude. He was an unexpected fusion of Barbadian and Canadian sensibilities, and something else–wholly credible. Franck easily trusted his honesty and confidence. "I may not find your grandmother, miss, but I will do all that I can," he said. Marsha liked him from the moment they met: slightly taller than she, he looked her in the eyes and laughed with genuine amazement at her stories about Nana's occasional yet extreme memory lapses. "Lemma tell yuh," she said, sounding like Paul Keens-Douglas live, "once she planted a whole kitchen garden and forget to water it. I admit this might be just another one of those senior moments for her, Julius, but to forget your only granddaughter? *Eh-eh.*"

There was a new concern in the detective's demeanour. He handed Marsha a photo. "Do you recognize that man?"

Marsha studied the five-by-seven digital print, shivered. The vivid hideousness of the dark surveillance-camera photo caught her off-guard. The man's face, which was partly hooded, was a bright purple and red, as if freshly bruised and bloodshot. His eyes were flame orange pixels, twin brimstones.

She handed the photo to Franck. He showed no reaction to the image and returned the photo to McDuff's desk, beside a worn hardcover copy of Caryl Phillips' *The Atlantic Sound.* "What about him?" he said, sitting back in his chair.

McDuff took a short breath. "There have been six ritual killings across Montreal in the last six months. All boy children, all black, all wealthy, all taken from their parents' homes at midnight on the nineteenth of each month. Then found literally butchered the next day. The police say it's a serial killer, but it's obvious we're dealing with something more sinister, which is the only reason, really, they invited me to join their investigation. Where we openly agree is that this man is involved." McDuff shifted the photo so the subject would face Franck. "So you recognize him."

"Yes," said Franck immediately, unprepared for the detective's redirect.

"But how is he involved in Nana's disappearance? You say he kills babies. Nana's cute, but no one would ever mistake her for cuddly."

"Your grandmother's kitchen table was full of clippings of the murders from all of the newspapers across the island. From what you've told me, and I can ascertain, she disappeared around the same time we—the police and I—somehow lost track of him."

"You know where he lives?" said Franck.

"Not quite," said McDuff, reclining in his chair. He turned back to Marsha. "There was no sign of forced entry at your grandmother's apartment. Her security cameras never went offline. The photo I showed you was from one of the victim's surveillance systems before he—"

Marsha was shaking her head at all this information. "Who—is—*he*?"

McDuff avoided looking at her. He now turned to Franck. "I was hoping you'd be able to tell me."

There was a long pause. Marsha watched Franck, and Franck held the detective's stare.

"My Aunt and Uncle used to rent a room to him when I was little. But he didn't look like that, and…." Franck stopped himself.

"And what?" said Marsha before McDuff could.

Franck was going to say the man he knew never killed babies, but somehow he understood: that this man *was* a killer all back then, *long* before then, and that may have been the only reason his Aunt and Uncle offered the brute shelter under their roof, with their young nephew, not because he was a hardworking Bajan in need of a warm place to stay while he made his way in a cold country. Instead, Franck settled on an only slightly more convincing lie:

"I never knew his real name. We called him 'Burt,' or 'Bart.' Never anything else. Nothing else."

They left the detective's office and caught the 110 bus below Pont Mercier to Angrignon metro. From there, they continued to ride in silence to Lionel-Groulx station, where they transferred to the Côte-Vertu line for a Vendôme bus to their motel, Le Chateau, at the bottom of St. Jacques. It was midday; most Montrealers were at work, and the buses would remain empty until school was out, around three in the afternoon. But it was only when they were en route to the motel that Marsha asked Franck: "So, spill it, nuh? What *weren't* you telling Julius?"

Franck smiled. He didn't think he had fooled her. They had no time for their customary coyness. And they weren't in Barbados anymore.

"Do you know who the Heart Man is?"

Marsha narrowed her eyes. "Isn't he one of our folk tales or something?"

"Oh, no, he was very real. The story Bajan mothers tell their children to scare them from wandering where they shouldn't is based on the St. Lucy murder of a young boy in a cave by two fishermen. They used the child's heart in a satanic ritual… they said for wealth, but it was really to stay young…."

Franck trailed off, Marsha prodded him. "So?"

"A white Bajan named Barton Springer hanged for the crime. His apprentice testified against him and was freed; the man eventually went mad. But there was another man mentioned, the one they said told them what to do, who was never found by the police. They said he rode a horse, but it was more likely a donkey–"

"How do you know all this?"

"Because: *that's* the story my Aunt and Uncle told me. Not the false one about some marauding, Syrian, beach bogeyman with a bloody scimitar who snatched children playing hooky. The *real* one. He's the man in McDuff's picture. None of this had anything to do with the Lodge–that was probably what he wanted us to think…. He's the one who got away. The Guardians must have been watching him–"

"The man in the picture," Marsha said, "even with his face looking the way it did, he couldn't be much older than you or me."

"No," agreed Franck, looking outside the bus' wide window. The Super C shopping centre came into view on his left then the Harvey's restaurant beyond it. He got up to ring the bell. "I guess, whatever they were doing in that cave, it worked for him."

The second they stepped into their motel room, the telephone rang. Franck and Marsha glanced at each other in the darkness. Only three people had their number, and a call from any of them could only be about one thing. Their first days in Montreal, they had expected to hear from Milton directly, but they were starting to understand what the Elders were already battling without having to deal with their desertion as well.

Franck picked up the receiver.

"Hullo? May I speak to the young lady, please?"

He handed it to Marsha with a shrug.

"So you finally come fuh she."

"Who is this?" she said.

"I see you at the detective's–recognize you from de pictures in the ole woman's flat. I was goin tuh make a meal of McDuff–he have a lot uh heart, dat one–but when I see you, young and strong, I *know* you is meant fuh me...."

"If you've hurt her–"

He dropped out of dialect but still sounded too familiar. "She thought she could stop me. She has nothing I want. You, though, have everything I *need*. A trade, then: meet me at a place called le Moulin Fleming–the old Scottish mill–on the border of LaSalle and Lachine. It's easy to find. Just above the detective's house on your right."

"When?"

"Tonight. At 11:30."

"And how am I to know it's you?"

Franck had been following the conversation. His eyes opened wide, and he shook his head at this. Marsha put up a hand.

"My features have grown quite distinct. You'll know it's me, darlin."

Marsha's blood crawled at the word.

"I'll be the one with your Nana."

"OK," she said.

"And leave yuh tour guide home. Franck always did like tuh mind big-people business tumuch."

He hung up.

29

David saw what looked like a woman waving at him. She was down by the bread-and-cheese tree, in the bend, opposite the Church of God. The street leading to Bourne's Land was dark, but she seemed to be dressed in white. There was enough light to make out her size and shape from the crossroads at Niles Corner. She was waving him her way, and he followed.

He had just come out of the Roy Smith shop holding an orange plastic bag of Anchor cheese, Sodabix, and four small Pine Hill boxed juices for Sashanna and him. A late snack, really, as they had had a supper of brown rice, fried flying fish, and a bit of cucumber. Sashanna's appetite was finally starting to return since the Sam Lord's incident.

She remembered little of the attack–or of her attacker–at the castle. But the duppy-dust or whatever it was Milton gave him to feed her couldn't stop the bad dreams. A few times in the early morning, when it was still dark, she woke him with her thrashing, as if trying to break free of her own buried memories.

Sashanna knew something had happened to her that day at the castle, just not exactly what. In careful conversations David had with her about how she was feeling, she seemed to believe she had been taken by a serial killer. Although Barbados, for many obvious reasons, had counted or convicted very few such monsters, Sashanna was not far wrong. What was a man who repeatedly lured ships to their wreck for his own gain and satisfaction? What was a spirit who would continue to do the same with people as his vessels?

David looked around him and saw that he had passed Douglas Shopping Centre without even realizing it. He had lost the orange bag he was holding. He now stood on the beach at Silver Sands, the shak-shak sound of the waves filling his ears. The woman in white was a distance from him in the misty moonlight. He became aware of her again with a start. She was coming toward him, and he was compelled to stay, wait for her to join him where he stood. She moved toward him as if on ice skates, figure skating. He noticed her footprints in the sand didn't match, as if she was barely touching the grains with her feet. And he wanted to know if she was like him: if she could fly and was hovering, as he sometimes did, slightly above the ground–because you could–or to remind yourself you could. He was warm with excitement.

Within six feet of the woman in white, Sashanna ran from behind a grassy sand dune with a charred almond branch. She swung with a grunt at the woman's head. There was a crack. The woman dropped. Sashanna stood over her, breathing hard. David stared at them, could not divide in his mind one from the other before she spoke.

"I start tuh get frighten in de house alone, so uh come out to meet yuh. When uh see yuh comin back, uh smile and call you name, but yuh look straight past me, drop de bag wid de food and walk off toward de sea. When uh get to de top of de gap, all uh see is dis woman yuh headin for–driftin, as if is me dreamin, and *nothin* I say can brek she spell." Sashanna stepped over the body, both hands on her stick and her eyes on the still form.

"I'm sorry," David said, slowly returning to himself. Time had felt normal to him, though he was vaguely aware that it wasn't. He was a sleepwalker awakened outside his own home.

"David, wha goan on here?"

"I don't know who she is, Sashanna, I swe–"

"No–*look*."

She pointed with the stick at the woman's left leg. It was hairy. Black as coal. Cloven. And she had a musty smell.

"The djablès," he said, and with far less surprise than Sashanna expected.

Her stick wavered. She started to cry. "I doan remember it all, but uh *know* somethin strange did happen tuh me at Sam Lord's. And now dis–*ting*–nearly tek you way from me. David, what in de hell is goan on?"

David took her hand with the stick. She released her grip on the weapon. "Hold on," he said, placing her arms firmly around his neck. He held her around the waist and looked up, into the sky.

The next moment, they were soaring like birds, racing like jets, across the coral moon.

30

Milton rested his copy of Jimmy Weatherhead's *Revelations* on his desk. It was dog-eared and scrawled up and barely held intact by its spine. The extensive markings and poor condition were merely for show. He had read the book in a very brief sitting and, naturally, needed no notes or arrows or underscores to highlight or recall themes, phrases, or plot points. He had found his young students took greater interest in a near-abused text than in a pristine one. It was as if the words couldn't be trusted until they were interrogated, attacked, hacked.

Despite his total recall, he reread "Chance Encounter," one of the collection's central stories. Milton described it to his class earlier that morning as prophetic.

"Do any of you believe we can see into the future?"

Only a few put their hands in the air. He waved them down. He was aware the average Barbadian could not perceive the beasts as they were, and certainly not in the day, though the beasts did not need to be seen to be felt. Law enforcement officers and politicians held press conferences to blame foreign elements and local vagabonds for the increase in unexplained disturbances in the land. There had been attacks at night on random districts in the country, and the disgusting vandalism with goats' blood of old Lodge buildings in St. Michael's Row and Roebuck Street in Bridgetown. Milton detected in all his students an anxiety that told him they suspected a wickedness was gradually erupting like a nest of red ants from the ground in Barbados.

"Thank you," he said. "I don't mean the kind of prophecy that says, 'This will happen then.' We're talking about the kind that suggests the shape of events unforeseen or barely glimpsed. That is often the power, magic, and beauty of art—the truth it reveals about humanity's situation–*despite* the artist. Here are some facts about the stories we have discussed by a man who simply was described as 'Noted Caribbean Author.'"

Of course, Milton knew Weatherhead was *more* than that. He was the Emissary. Such an individual–if he existed–was often not obvious; he was well hidden, though it was not clear to Milton– from Weatherhead's stories or the man's life–how much of his role in the current Cataclysm the Noted Caribbean Author understood. Not even Weatherhead would have been prepared to read his own work in this way. He was a fiction writer and an essayist whose stories were not ranked among humanity's greatest. Milton hadn't tried to convince his students of Weatherhead's deserved elevation; instead, he pointed out what should have been obvious: that Weatherhead wrote about how lives lived moment by moment in the Caribbean are redeemed by individual action. Naipaul's unflinching eye as a novelist was no less Weatherhead's, different in style and renown as the two writers were.

"'Chance Encounter,'" Milton said, "hinted at the need for unity and camaraderie among peoples, and at the decline of such a pursuit. All the old conflicts were there: between rich and poor, country and city, excitement and complacency, including a warning: what seduces as a child, learn to reconcile as man. Opposites must attract and destroy–or be destroyed–for order to exist."

Milton also knew "Chance Encounter" was a red herring, a sprat cast to catch a whale, as one of Weatherhead's characters might say. "If Memory Serves" held the message. He turned to the first page of the story and did something he hadn't done in, he guessed, well over three score and ten years. He chuckled. A student had tried in the earlier class to make a case for the story's greater import. Poorly.

"But sir, I think–" the boy began.

"Understand this," Milton crossed him, "now and until you leave my tutelage: I am not interested in what you *think*. I am interested in the *truth*. Entertain me with that, and I may yet let you finish a sentence in my class."

The other students had laughed. The boy took the upbraiding with a retiring sigh, sinking back into his seat.

Sometimes, Milton feared he was becoming as callous as Machiavelli the longer he remained in this form. Whether or not, "If Memory Serves" was the story. And Weatherhead's last column, "Imprimatur." "If Memory Serves" reflected the obeah women, the Elders, and their encounter with each other. Milton saw in that work the disintegration of societies and the dying of a world and the fire that would re-ignite it, and where the spark came from: the Caribbean.

"Mr. Francis in the story is so like Barbados and her people: as complacent as black belly sheep… yet trying to find a way as they butt about. Never mind Weatherhead's claim 'If Memory Serves' is about the decline of a Barbadian calypsonian he knew. He misread the climax of his own stories when they were this subtle. The songs buried in Mr. Francis' cellar become the beasts born of shadows. Weatherhead may have been trying to dismiss them, ignore them and the ones he saw already within his own land, but he couldn't."

Milton paused. He noted to himself one of the obeah women was missing from the story; the one who was familiar to him. As if she didn't belong. Black Cat was not conjured or invoked; that's what he felt in her presence, in her eyes. "Yet so powerful?" he asked himself. What mirror image did the Elect have of themselves? Would they find the vision Mr. Francis in the story claims to lack? Would they learn what light truly was? Or would they succumb to confusion? The answers to these questions were never clear.

Milton had underlined key phrases and words in the final story, "Neither Here Nor Home":

"'…. Even so,'" he continued, "'strange as it seemed, it was left to outsiders to remind locals of what they already knew.… Of course, the players had the power of myth I had come to expect, if not fully accept.… The choice could never be mine as someone so young.… Their presence here and today could only be coincidence, but the kind a man came to understand with time and patience as a grand accident, meaning no accident at all.… Life was little longer than cane season, cut short either by cutlass or by fire.… Although briefly in league, those few hours or days were enough to link our hearts, lighten our souls, connect us and others through us.…'"

Milton stopped his scanning.

"Note the repetition to the quartet of stories, a replaying of each other's finer points. Weatherhead grappled as much with form as with content."

But to be fair, Milton thought to himself, the Emissary could not know how to interpret his own work's subversion.

"Like Naipaul, sometimes his short stories read like personal essays; sometimes his personal essays read like short stories. Yet, again like Naipaul, he could be admired for his elaborate, deceptively digressive detail, forgiven for its piercing perception of the things that mattered most to people."

Needlessly, Milton checked his timepiece. "That's enough." He stopped talking and sat down, observing and stroking its face. Students trickled past him, then they poured out of the room. When the last had drained away, Milton locked the doors on both sides of the auditorium simultaneously.

If Weatherhead was right, he now realized, the Elect had barely three weeks to dispel the beasts.

31

Franck stood in the shadow of the railway bridge at the end closest the restored windmill. The tall wood-and-stone structure, built in 1827 by a Scotsman on the shore of the St. Lawrence, reminded him of the ruined monoliths that dotted Barbados. Only the Morgan Lewis Mill, exactly a hundred years older, was still in operation as a tourist attraction. Moulin Fleming's stationary sails once ground grain, not cane, but there was little difference in outward design between it and its 18th-century cousin.

There were other similarities between Barbados and this coastal area, such as galvanized fencing, permaclad roofing, bridges, and many churches. Franck felt uneasy. In coming to Montreal, he and Marsha had travelled from one island to another. It was as if they were on the Heart Man's turf, not theirs. High school history lessons and bicycle trips up and down the shore had taught him this was where the first settlers to the New World came, and First Nation people showed them how to trap, fish, stay warm... basically, stay alive. These were ancient grounds whose meaning or power to those who now lived here has never been fully appreciated. Franck doubted the mill was an arbitrary choice for the Heart Man.

"If you don't have a plan," his Aunt and Uncle used to tell him, "then the only plan you have is to fail." They had come up with a plan. Looking around him, Franck was less and less sure it would work.

Marsha was stationed outside the metal door to the mill, on the lookout beneath dark grey trees. Below her was LaSalle Boulevard, quiet and low-lit. Below that, the rushing St. Lawrence. She didn't know anything more about the Heart Man than Franck could recall, but she doubted he could survive being pelted into its frigid water with the force of a battering ram.

The Heart Man slipped out of a shadow. Nana was beside him and shackled.

Marsha stepped toward him, fists clenching. "The plan," Franck whispered. "Stick to the plan."

She released her fists. "So you're here."

"We all are," he said, sniffing the air. Unlike in the photo McDuff showed her, the Heart Man wore no hood. His hands were a deep purple, and his face was blotched as if with sorrel and blue-soap. He wasn't a tall man or big. Average looking, except for his skin. Franck had told her he petrified his prey with the beat of all the hearts he had stolen. Marsha checked herself. Her heart ran steady.

"Give her to me," she said, stretching out her arms.

"Eh-eh, Trini-Gal. *You* first." He tightened his grip on Nana's chains, and she fell to her knees whimpering. Her eyes shot up at Marsha, moved back and forth. Not in pain or fear, but in defiance... warning. She was ordering Marsha: "No."

Marsha held back. "Why take her?" she said. "I thought the heart of an old woman wasn't so precious to you."

"She came after me!" The Heart Man beat his chest. "Claimed unfinished business. And we both know she ain't no old lady."

"I want her back."

"And I wanna go Home, darlin. I come to Canada because it de *last* place anybody would look for me. Not England. Not de States. Where better to lose meself–hop-sa-sa–than where there're *nuff* West Indians *and* no one would look? And if them did, there was still the Circle of the Grand Order.... Y'hear me now? *The. Cir. Cle.* The two of we had a bargain. You know dat? I side wid dem, and I's invisible to creature-keepers.... Yuh hear? Like Franck's creature-keepers... and her! Hop-sa-sa! But is now time to re*turn.*"

Her Nana's eyes again. Alarmed.

"You're not leaving this place," said Marsha. The Heart Man started to pulse and shine.

"You would *stop* me, darlin? You ain't got the hearts."

Marsha charged him. He changed Nana's chains from his right hand to his left, unwrapping them. She saw it all as if in bullet time, but not his open backhand. She was sent crashing through the mill's door.

"See what I mean?" he said. The Heart Man threw Nana's chains around the mill's sails. From a sheath on his back, he pulled a curved cutlass.

Marsha swayed in the doorway, trying to catch her breath. The blow *hurt*–actually hurt her, not just stung. She tasted her own blood.

He advanced, and she tried to take a step back before she realized there was no room to dodge him in the narrow visitor's foyer.

"You're sturdier than you look. That shoulda whip off your head."

"You want my heart... you come... get it...."

"A pleasure, darlin. Always a pleasure."

He leapt at her with the sword. Marsha jumped the staircase to the mill's second floor.

Franck was up the incline to the mill and beside Nana in a second. McDuff emerged from where he hid among the silent trees.

Franck tried the locks and chains.

"Step back," McDuff said. He took his revolver from its holster and fired three quick shots at the chains above her head. The manacles fell away. Nana dropped into Franck's arms. "I couldn't let him go," she said to him. "I couldn't! He was waiting... *between* worlds...."

"How do we kill it?" said McDuff.

A section of the third-floor exploded. Franck saw it as it happened: the cracks in the wall, the shooting bricks, and Marsha, battered bloody, tumbling amid the debris. He moved between the falling missiles to catch her. He felt a hand around the back of his neck. Then nothing at all.

"Not so fast now, eh, boy? I told her not to bring yuh. You was never as strong as the others."

The Heart Man tossed his body against the side of the mill.

McDuff emptied his gun into the beast's chest. He buckled then rose.

"Bullets can't *kill* me," he said, moving toward McDuff.

"I know," McDuff said. "But now she can."

With a sound like mud hitting a wall, Marsha thrust her right hand through the Heart Man's back. She raised him off the ground, a lizard on a pin, feet and arms dangling, head twitching. The smell of mould oozed from the cavity.

"Darlin," the Heart Man gasped at the arm jutting through his chest.

She gripped his heart in her hand, an organ of many massed into one. Vivid blue, red and purple, it pulsed with hunger. Marsha squeezed until it burst and her nails dug into the palm of her hand.

32

Daren John watched the tops of the trees as he paddled through Graeme Hall's waters toward the coast. The boat had a motor, but he preferred slow progress to any disturbance his presence might attract. The sanctuary was closed. He was obviously trespassing, though it wasn't so long ago the area was open to hikers and wanderers, if they could stand the sulphurous stench of the waters. Daren glanced at the bow of the boat. Wrapped in a clear plastic net at his feet was a slim, pink baccou, no more than three and a half feet tall. The tufts of hair on its head were milk white, and its dark red eyes were huge. The beast's thickly muscled arms were pinned against its chest, like a bat's.

The full moon shone brightly behind powdery blue clouds. Barbados at night took on a life that could only be seen in certain light.

The island's first prime minister might have navigated this same way, sucking on that Cuban cigar, motioning to his cronies, *Quiet, men. You'll scare way the fowls.* Laughing, sweating and smiling. Already savouring the gamy taste of the bird as he took aim, cocked his gun, squinted, exhaled and fired, his cheeks trembling but his arms steady. One of Daren's mentors, a tribal leader and certainly not one of the politician's cortege, used to tell him the stories. So many stories, he couldn't possibly have witnessed every one even if he had been that close. But he told them as if he had been there, every time. His mentor had lived a long, long life.

Daren knew: the island's first prime minister never hunted the kind of beasts he was after tonight. If he did, the soldier in him was stronger than the politician. He never told a soul. Not his wife, nor any mistress....

Daren's mentor had no fear of such revelations. He knew all the possible theories for and about Barbados' existence, all the legends and myths and misinformation upon which the country was based–even how the coral island really got its name. He–all the tribal leaders–knew its wildlife and plantlife, its medicines and poisons, its fable beasts by name and folk lore, the souls of its black slaves and white slaves, African queens and European princes, what still thrived in its canes and what was long extinct, or close to it, in its caves. He knew which peoples, how many more than the three usually cited, had built up the island, and which had left their mark, which were deliberately forgotten. All this knowledge was in the soil, in its centuries of sediment, and all this Daren was expected someday to know and pass on.

The boat reached the shore. Daren dragged the baccou out by the rope around its chest. The beast seemed heavier than when Daren tied it up and lifted it in. Daren stopped to study it. It did not resist him, but its eyes were as wide as sand dollars, its pupils small as tamarind seeds, and it was grinning up at the hunter and beyond him.

Daren dropped the baccou at his feet and reached for the knives strapped to his ribs. The shapes of the trees, the shadows they cast, and the smell of the swamp had changed. There was an absence of sound, as if the crickets and whistling frogs and night birds in the swamp had died.

One beast appeared in the trees then another. Then another and another and another, breathing fast and shallow, their eyes staring. Leering at him, they held bloody shards of coral stones in bloody hands. Not just one baccou or ten or twenty, as he had known was possible–but dozens upon dozens of them in the trees, like gangs of green monkeys. A wall of baccous, crashing toward him.

Daren turned. He ran for the boat.

The first rock hit him like a cannonball in the back of his left knee, shattering it. Daren dragged himself up, knives still in hand. Four rocks, one after the other, bludgeoned his back. Something snapped.

It was true, Daren said to himself as the baccous approached him, hands in the air—he thought of playing football with other boys in his village, watching his mother make cornmeal bakes for breakfast, hiking and fishing with his father and his father's brothers, hunting with the tribal leaders, the first time he was with Nina, the birth of their child, and how he would miss watching Corrie grow into a man—in seconds, he witnessed his own life, and then the rockstones fell from above.

He came soon after the beasts had retreated into the trees, flung themselves back to their crab holes, his stick in one hand and medicine pouch in the other, but too late. Too late? He would not have stood long against the baccous, either. He had never arrived too late, in plenty or in time of need. He often heard the drumming of the tuk band before he appeared—at least he used to. Now? The only voice he heard was that of the people. He put the medicine pouch into one of the pockets that bulged his pants.

Daren, the Hunter, was dead, broken by the beasts he was sworn to subdue. But there had been so many of them. Something was different. Something had *changed*. Consciousness had always come suddenly. He was here, and he acted, and then he was no longer necessary. Until the next time. He raised his stick. Something *had* changed. He could see it in the skies, his stars, as he lifted the body of the Hunter over his shoulder and watched the tree line not long ago filled with monsters.

Something had changed. Consciousness came, just as suddenly; shirt, shorts, sandals, stick, and spirit, all that he was.

But more than himself was still here.

Mackie walked along the rubble unseen by most of the duppies. There were many trapped bodies. Some were dead, killed the moment the planes struck, some were slowly dying. He could do nothing for them, and they knew this—he was not any angel they had expected to encounter—and the area grew silent as souls slipped passed him and away.

What had drawn him here? Something was wrong—all the dead, the duppies, pinned to this site. Milton should be here, he thought, not him. Unless, now, after all that had occurred, *he* should be.

Mackie rose above the noxious debris, above moans and supplication, into the dust-filled, jet-fuelled air, swirling like a hurricane. And the stony city crouched below him like a giant on bended knee was fatally hobbled. There was a saying he had heard from old Bajans, often flung at their proud-foolish young: "Yuh start wrong, yuh gine end wrong."

He could barely glimpse what had changed from this vantage point: the fast one was gone, and then so was the Hunter, and all these souls lost, and more beasts to come....

Mackie looked down at the wreckage, and his eyes became wet. *He was crying.* Actual, real tears. When was the last time he cried? He couldn't remember… it didn't matter. A previous life—a million lifetimes ago. It never mattered, except that now he cried.

End of Part 2

PART 3

We don't have magic power....
We cannot order anyone around, but our
power is in argument and persuasion.

Chinua Achebe, BBC News, 2002

33

There was a chill in the tropical night air as David flew to the east coast. The coolness was clinging, like cold spots in the sea on mornings after the sun was up long enough to warm some of the water but not all. Turbulence caused his stomach to be uneasy, which was a troubling sensation. He had always been immune to the effects of wind, friction, pressure, and temperature when flying.

Growing up, David was not allowed to fly in open spaces. He understood. It was forbidden to be seen doing so by others. Theophilus and Huldah made that clear, even without the nursery-rhyme warning. It would be a problem for all of them: for those who saw David and for his family. So he found an empty pasture at the island's northern tip, in the parish already said to be behind God's back—and certainly behind his Guardians'—to test his wings. The pasture was dry, with white stones sticking out of the earth like broken bones. Black belly sheep grazed on the horizon and after that nothing: the sky, the sun, space, and more space. He closed his eyes, stretched out his arms, and rose into the air, into all that openness. It was different from flying in the house or Theophilus' forge, and he knew it would be, which was why he wanted to do it—had to do it. He breached the troposphere, then the stratosphere, then the mesosphere—he knew when he had exceeded an upper limit, even though he didn't know the names for them at the time. He felt like a superhero, a god, indescribably powerful and freed by Nature. Racing like a rocket, David only slowed when he reached the thermosphere, the last layer before outer space.

He knew he could fly to the moon and back, and all in a cyc-ling suit and hoodie. Yet here he was shivering slightly. His parents called anything less than twenty-five degrees Celsius cold—in

December or January. It was late October, and temperatures were in the low teens. The world was changing around him. Changing? Things were falling apart, and despite what Milton told him about what had happened to Marsha and Franck, poor Franck, he really didn't understand why.

David looked down, searching among the simple board-and-shingle shacks Bajans owned as vacation homes or rented to surfers. He found nothing refreshing about the air he breathed, once (and still by many) believed to be a cure-all. The Atlantic was ripping and rocky, and a few lights lit kitchens or bedrooms. He followed a strip of land cut between the road and the sea that marked where the General Railway last ran a locomotive. Barbados was one of many islands in the Caribbean to have trains, though bad maintenance eventually caused the company to fail in 1934. David pictured the elegant black and white photos he saw from the period at the museum. It seemed all the women dressed heavily in white, the men in dark woollen suits, and no one smiled for the cameras. From Bridgetown to Carrington or Bathsheba to Belleplaine, people could get there by train. This was bizarre to him and probably to the travellers of the day: trains as public transportation were what England had, or Canada, or America, to travel long, wide distances, not a place as small or narrow as Barbados.

Up ahead, David saw Milton hailing him. David hovered above, not too close to the ground.

"Sir," he called out.

Milton nodded, looking up.

"I'm glad you got my message. I missed you after class today."

"I wasn't really up to hanging around."

"To tell the truth, neither was I."

Milton rose from the sandy ground into the sky beside David.

"Fly with me?"

David shrugged and began to drift away over the ocean. Milton followed.

"It's hard to appreciate the east coast at night like this. Areas that look as pretty as any prairie or forest become nothing but dark patches by moonlight."

"What did you want to talk to me about, sir?"

Milton turned to him as they floated through the sky, higher into the clouds.

"Franck is gone; and Marsha is still away, her light low. There will be further consequences to their actions here in Barbados. I wanted to know how *you* are doing. You must feel very alone–"

"I'm not. I have Sashanna."

"Your girlfriend. Yes. And how is she?"

"She's better."

"I see she knows," Milton said. David watched him, his lips tightening. "Sorry. It was not so difficult to read. It is foremost on your mind."

After a moment, David said, "I wish she didn't know."

Milton considered his words. "In time, if you live long enough, you will understand that the truth is seldom a complicating factor. Is a true prophet someone who says what is not known, or that person who knows what simply hasn't been said?"

"You called Weatherhead the second kind of prophet."

"I did, didn't I? You've been paying attention."

David finished his thought: "You're saying Weatherhead some-how knew about us, our... coming?"

"Yes. But much of what happens in existence has happened before. Not in some other time or reality, but in our own. There are elements in the universe I still wonder about...." Milton stared at David. "Don't look so shocked, boy. I am not what you would like to think I am."

"Theophilus, one of my Guardians, told me it's our demons that drive us to excel and angels that save us from ourselves."

Milton nodded. "That sounds like something Theo would say, especially in a moment of casual reflection."

"You knew him?"

"I knew them all... but you needn't fear, David–if that is your fear: neither I nor Mackie is either of those. What you call God is not responsible, here. Humanity is. Humanity caused the Cataclysm. Humanity must fix it."

David slowed when they came to a thick mist. He could not see the stars above. He had lost track of the moon. "I don't understand," he said. "But I want to."

"Then ask me what you really want to know."

David hesitated before saying, "Why us? Why now?"

Milton shook his head.

"You won't answer my questions?"

"Not when you already know the answers." They stopped to rest on a cloud. "A Cataclysm is not about who or when. It only happens if the appearance of evil in the world is unambiguous and too strong to be left unchecked. And there are always three Elect–three sacrifices–who must act as one."

"And now there are only two," David said, folding his arms.

"So it seems," said Milton. "The beasts of Barbados' legends and myths will gradually displace the Known World. The two, the Known and the Unknown, cannot exist in equal measure or form. Your world is *already* dying."

"So *we* must stop them–*if* Marsha comes back–"

"Correct, though your number is unprecedented."

"–by making a 'sacrifice' of ourselves."

"Yes."

"But we're not Americans. Why not them? They've got the weapons and an army–"

Milton smiled.

"Because it's your time."

"It's our time?" David repeated it as a question. Milton sighed.

"Sometimes, humans think that because a people are an obvious power that they are a necessary power, when truly that people's position is trivial. 'They also serve those who stand and wait.'"

David refused to take on the reference. "We're just students. This has nothing to do with us–"

Milton's eyes crackled. "*Many* people from *many* countries have already died because of the Cataclysm. You're human beings, who have been given great power for a purpose. Is it any more foolish to believe you, Marsha, and Franck could save this world, the little you know of it and the rest you don't, than a farm boy from Kansas?"

David stared at Milton trying not to laugh. "That was a story."

"And this, too, will be a story–is already–to many. They all are, my boy."

David was quiet. What Milton was saying made some sense to him yet at the same time seemed too big to contemplate during this discussion in the sky. Milton moved closer to him, to look into his eyes. The Elder's own had calmed from their fiery hazel of a moment ago to a softer colour David had never known was possible. He dared one last question.

"Who were our parents?"

"Theophilus and Huldah–"

"Our *real* parents."

Milton paused.

"It may be I don't understand your question. In all the ways that matter, whether you called them aunt, uncle, father, mother, or grandmother, the Guardians were your parents."

"They couldn't have given birth to us."

"No one could have."

David's mouth slowly opened, but he didn't know how to respond.

"What are you trying to prove, David?" asked Milton.

"That we weren't spawned."

"Far from! You came from Nature. You belong to Nature."

"But not to our Guardians... biologically."

"You shared—as we all do—the same DNA."

"How—?"

"They were your parents."

"Who are all dead, now."

"But you know that everything dies—almost."

"You're not going to tell me *how* Marsha, Franck, or I got here, or from where—are you?"

Milton shook his head. "Tell me this: Did you—or any of the others—ever feel the Guardians *didn't* love you... as parents?"

David didn't need to think about it: "No."

"Then the only thing I have to tell you is that, as unwilling or incapable as you are of believing it right now, we in the Caribbean can save the world if we want to."

"You talk as if you're one of us," David shot back.

Milton was briefly stunned. He had been born human again and of this region for all of three months. It had been, he discovered, long enough.

"Right now, at this moment, I am," he said. "The one difference is that the choice to do something with it belongs to you young Elect."

34

Julius C. McDuff drove his roadster through the Motel Cavelier's entrance and up to Room 26. He switched off the heat and turned off the engine and killed the headlights, and sat and waited awhile in the dissipating warmth. He was sure Marsha had heard and seen him. No lights came on, either outside or inside the room. He sucked his teeth and stepped out of the cooling car into the cold night air.

Marsha had moved into one of the cheaper motels on the other side of the street. With its dollar-store décor and strong-smelling little soaps and blue-movie cable TV, it was a transient place. But she had no desire to go anywhere.

She was almost completely recovered from her fight with the Heart Man. Faster, McDuff thought, than he believed it would take even given her injuries. She had minor cuts and bruises. She acted as if she would die. "Omuhgod–I'm bleedin?–I'm *actually bleedin*," she kept saying back at his office, holding her side with one hand and feeling her face with the other. She told McDuff she had been surprised at being winded keeping up with Franck, at feeling her flesh opening up and seeping when struck by the Heart Man. She wasn't invulnerable–she assumed as much, right?–but she was always strong, resilient... against mere mortals. She laughed at that. She was really playin in she own league now, boy, she told him. Leapin tall buildings in a single bound wouldn't cut it when David was able tuh soar like a angel. It took McDuff's best bedside manner to get enough painkillers into her so she might rest. He worried he might be trying to sedate an elephant with an aspirin. McDuff didn't know who David was, either, but believed, after what he had seen, that there must be a man somewhere out there who could indeed fly.

So, physically, Marsha was fine.

"It's Julius." McDuff knocked on the door.

"Come in," a faint voice called back.

It was her battered pride that needed mending.

Marsha lay on the bed in the room with no lights on and the blinds drawn. She was flat on her back on top of the sheets, dressed in grey cotton tights with stripes down either side and a white tank top. A pillow half-covered her face.

"I spoke with Serge–Sergeant Delvecchio. He'll see Nana's and Franck's bodies are released to me. There's no one else to claim them, anyway. Correct?"

He waited for an answer. When she said nothing, he continued.

"I'm making funeral arrangements for both of them. I'll need help with some of the details."

He waited for an answer before approaching the bed.

"You should get up," he said.

"You should go away."

"I want to help you–"

"You can't," she said.

"Then tell me who can."

"There's no one."

McDuff stood back. Marsha didn't move; even her chest barely rose and fell with her breathing.

"I don't believe you," he said and turned away from her. McDuff took off his leather jacket, folded it over his left arm, and sat in the chair by the window beside a little round table.

"Do angels exist?" she said as if to him. "I thought they were angels. I wanted them to be. I was foolish to think they could exist. Franck didn't…."

She pinched the cross around her neck, rubbing the metal.

"Is that what you believed?"

"I don't know." Pause. "Yes."

McDuff didn't know who she was talking about.

"But they weren't," he said.

Pause.

"No," Marsha answered. "They weren't."

35

The avengers were assembled. Anansi, the Man-Spider, whose body kept jumping from one animal form to the next—first Snake then Tiger then Monkey then Parrot—all the animals of his storied kingdom, quickly, like a looping black-and-white film reel. Beside him was Mr. Harding, burning—a human torch, severe in crocus bag pants, waistcoat, and top hat: eyes ablaze, puffing smoke each time he spoke, every breath the smell of burnt bagasse. No other light but his lit the cave. These beasts craved less light, never more. The duppies in the stalactites and stalagmites were rowing. They, too, demanded to know when they would be completely unfettered. Shaggy Bear, armoured in a vest of multicoloured, diamond-hard shells, his massive arms and legs sheathed in sharp, singed, crystallized banana fronds, told them to be quiet—QUIET—*he* was presiding over this meeting, which would be their last before their return to the Known World.

And the baccous banged their rocks in a riot against the ground, causing the duppies in the stalactites and stalagmites to wince. But the loin-clothed, red-eyed, pale-skinned goblins beat out a chattering, triumphant rhythm, as if playing mas. Shaggy Bear nodded deeply, acknowledging their victory.

After the stoning of Prince Daren, the Hunter, the first of his First Nation, fear spread across the island. Maybe there were baccous hunting humans, as sightings suggested (the Bear held up with his right paw a newspaper turned to the editorial page), and that runaway ox was a steel donkey after all (the Bear held up with his left paw the back-page story of another newspaper). The steel donkey, snorting fire and coal, clanging like a choir of pots, reared on musty grey hind legs and phased in and out of visibility. Other strange occurrences reported included visitations by vexed spirits claiming former great houses and plantations as their own (the well-known Chase vaults and other tombs were in a mess, coffins upended and open), and men claiming to be lured, stalked, by a hauntingly beautiful Creole woman dressed in white and smelling of stale sea salt.

Mr. Harding cracked his whip, giving off sparks. His beloved cousin the Hag stood beside him, her torso a ball of liquid fire, her blood boiled to make her skin translucent. Yet she was lovelier than her younger sister, La Djablès, who called up the waves in the cave, and the waves crashed against the cave walls. The duppies in them shuddered. Family smiled at family with fanged teeth. The baccous cracked the earth with their rocks. Good, good, good, they banged. It is time, time, time–

And the Bear roared. And the cave shook from its coral foundations. And all went quiet, quiet, quiet above and below ground for untold distances around.

The Bear looked over the assembled like a war lord, with fiery eyes.

They were far from Bridgetown, he reminded them, in that parish said to be behind God's back. And that northernmost parish *was* partly so hidden, being at an angle in the Caribbean Sea seldom surveyed by Her scouts. But they would be storming the city soon. Soon, there would be no need to hide in these dead zones, avoiding detection or interference.

The Elect were on the fence–or guard wall–undecided. They weren't so bright. One had even been defeated away from their protective shores. There was a doubtful whizzy-whizzying. It's true, *true,* the Bear growled. Thanks to the Heart Man, who was, regrettably, undone by a member of the Elect far stronger than Rachel Pringle ever was. Those of you who knew the formidable madam, innkeeper, and rum-shop owner would recall her power lay in more than her long, soft hair and pretty eyes.

Sam Lord and the Heart Man clapped and winked at this. They were shades of their former selves, reanimated as duppies at the behest of the inner column of the Circle of the Grand Order, who had become as mad and rogue as the beasts they helped loose. Now, both seen and unseen, these spirits could only observe. They could no longer engage the Known World. Their time had passed but not their usefulness. Both beat time to the Bear's words, one with his fist, the other with his heart, to a musical madness: papapa-*pa*, papa-*papa*, papa-*PAPA*.

There was only one other who *would* have hindered us, the Bear resumed, one who was once like us: a beast of beauty and myth birthed in the coral chasms of this Caribbean Sea. He pointed to the saltwater bubbling beneath Mr. Harding's feet. But this other one is no longer like us. The defeat of that one Elect changed him, pulled him into the knowledge of the Known World.

The Bear raised his tree-trunk arms with the two puny papers in hand. We will not be put back into the bottle. He flung the yellowed pages over the assembled; the baccous went wild. Too long have *we* been enslaved by humankind's limited imagination. We will show them what it means for us to be truly alive in their hearts and minds. We will march on Bridgetown, Barbados and then the rest of the Known World. Soon, it will be *our* time in the sun.

36

"It hurt, being hit by him...."

Marsha said this so softly McDuff thought he was dreaming.

"I never knew such creatures–'beasts,' the Elders call them–could exist. In real life, I mean. Franck was right; I've taken everything for granted. My strength, and my faith...."

McDuff lowered his feet from the little round table to sit straight. It was dark outside, but lightening on the horizon in that slow, grey way it did during late autumn months across Montreal, warmth seeping its way back into the world. He could see clouds or smoke filling the sky above the motel's neon sign. Clouds, he corrected himself with assurance. One look around reminded him of where he was, of what was a dream and what was reality. He rubbed his eyes with the back of his right hand and checked the time on his pocket watch. When he spoke, he saw his breath and shivered.

"I've seen many creatures in the Underworld I patrol. Only a few resembled the Heart Man."

"That explains a lot," she said. "You don't seem at all offset by any of this. Are you sure *you're* not an Elder?"

"No," he said, recognising some of her familiar banter, "I'm just a detective."

"That's good," she said. "To know. I'd hate to think you would let me get beat up so, if you were one. I'd have to at least try to kick the crap out of you for that."

"But you fought him. You won."

"Won? Won what? Without Franck, or me Nana.... There's no eighth samurai, Julius. We really screwed up."

Marsha turned her head slightly in McDuff's direction.

"You don't get it, do you? *Franck-was-right.* I never–in all my life–felt *pain* like I did when the Heart Man struck me. I never knew I *could*–never ever *suspected* it–and it scared me... *terrifies* me...."

".... There are more like him." McDuff was starting to understand.

".... Yes. God, yes. They've promised us a whole islandful if we don't do the right thing...." She wiped her eyes quickly with both hands. "I thought coming here was the right thing to do. To rescue Nana? We couldn't even rescue ourselves. And if the Lodge *is* involved, then what?"

McDuff glanced at her. Marsha had said little else about Franck or herself than what she rambled on about after she fought the Heart Man, and he had little more to go on than the story she and Franck first came to him with, which seemed true enough. Yet McDuff was growing certain about a couple of things.

"Do you know what you are?" he asked her.

"They tell me a saviour."

"Then you're like the Heart Man."

"What?!" she said, almost rising. "How could you–" she stopped.

McDuff explained: "You don't belong here. Do you?"

He heard her begin to sob.

Car doors opened and slammed in the motel's narrow parking lot. A yellow light edged the clouds with a faint glow. McDuff searched the room with his eyes for the thermostat.

"I want to see Nana," she said through sniffles. "And Franck. Can you do that?"

"Yes," McDuff said, and then he got up to turn on the heat.

37

He crossed the bridge at Bush Hall and walked down into Bank Hall. Past the traffic lights and rum-shops, past the bakery and slaughterhouse, the young and the old, the well off and the barely holding on. Down from one community to the next, from church to hardware, mango tree to clammy-cherry trunk, pasture to manor, cart road to upholsterer's shed. Down. Down. He journeyed across a next set of lights, into Eagle Hall, toward the open air market smelling of soft soursops, burst sugar apples, young shaddocks and earthy dunks, and beyond there, past the rotisserie and defunct dealerships, police station, fishcake and coconut vendor. Service station. Psychiatric hospital. Doctors and dentists and madmen and prostitutes. Men and women. All.

He had been wandering for seven days and seven nights since he emerged from the swamp with the broken body of the Hunter. He lay him in the middle of the highway, so no one would mistake him for a fallen-down drunk, not even the police at Worthing Sub-Station, and began to walk along the coast. But at the Garrison Savannah he turned right, followed the road, turned right, followed the road, turned right, followed…. He seemed to be heading somewhere, somewhere he hoped he would be needed. (Why else would he be called there, led there?)

Ho-hoy!
Hard ears
A bread an two
Gimme all, den
Tek em
What part Mama?

Up in she stall
To nasty up
Yuh blinkin idiot
Stinkin liar
Tief
Not one blind cent
Chippin
Left, right, left, right....

People were born different all the time. Different didn't mean special. But he was born to understand the spirit of his people, to know if they needed him and when. If she liked him. Or he liked her. He could tell. He could always tell a thing like that. Not quite what people were thinking but what they were feeling. He could reveal to his people their own hearts: their hopes, dreams, fears, and desires. Now they were all mashed up, brek up, then. Senseless. Confused.

Wunnuh doan know
You was
Big up
Soft soft
Got de belly
Pissy
Fraid for?
Frighten she
Boysie... No Bosie... Bo
Waxpalax
I hear yuh
Ram off
(Igrunt brute)

Dem parros
Black bitch
Suckabubbies
Dah she pram
Scratch off

The stick he carried dangled from his right hand. He folded it under his left arm. Walked on.

There were some things he still understood about himself.

He had been a keeper, a watcher, a waiter. The type of man (though not of men) who would say, "Good evenin, brown-skinned girl," and mean it, innocently. Who could defeat a shopful of armed youths to the riddim of their own heartbeat. Who could be counted on to know the right thing and do the right thing because it was the right thing.

He was one of the best (though not of the best). Before the swamp and the Hunter's death by more baccous than he had thought possible to dream or imagine. He was, then.

What was he now?

Fuh real
Talk a roll
Watch yuh pictures
Bush tea!
Whitepeople
Weblackpeople
Paling
Pompasetting
Nabel string
Breed me?!
Uh gone

Blue vex
Wha happen?
Tumuch
Tings
Brown
Real dread
A jockey... a lif up...
Yesplease
Go long
Ain't see you
In donkey years
Not like she
Jus de other day

Down from Black Rock, he faced Spring Garden Highway, past the shipping and furniture factory. He crossed the highway. Walked east again, toward Bridgetown, along a shoulder littered with sun-dried crapauds, their yellow bellies turned toward the sky. He saw a broken-boned, water-coloured, eight-sided kite dangling from a power line, and beneath the line the sign: De Gateway Café. Down. Down. Down by the sea.

He held his stick. He smoothed the neck of his white collarless shirt and felt the pockets of his three-quarter pants for coin, finding inside them twine, bundled herbs, a pocket-knife, notebook and pencil, and finally silver dollars. This was how he found himself, how he came to know himself, here, during his long walk down, which was not at all hot to him (though he was not unaware of the heat): dressed like a plainclothes police without a precinct, or like one whose precinct might be all of Barbados.

38

Sergeant Delvecchio let Marsha and McDuff into the morgue. He switched on the lights, and even Marsha had to squint a little until her eyes adjusted. There were rows upon rows of drawers in the room. She stepped further into the room ahead of the cop and the detective.

Sergeant Delvecchio held McDuff by the arm. "Jules. Are you sure she is ready for this?" he whispered.

McDuff nodded. Sergeant Delvecchio shrugged.

"Then let's go," he said, showing the way like a waiter in a restaurant. "Who would you like to see first?"

"My friend... Franck," Marsha said. Her voice sounded hollow in the room, which seemed a chamber between chambers, not a destination of its own.

"That one. Over there," he said. He pointed to a drawer with a number on it. He stood in front of it. "I should warn you–"

She cut him off. "No need," she said. She stared at him with sleepy eyes. Her hands were in the pockets of her grey sweat shirt as if she was cold. "I was there. Remember?"

Sergeant Delvecchio's lips twitched. He glanced at McDuff, whose eyes barely moved from Marsha, then he observed the girl one last time. "Eh bien," he said. He pulled open the drawer.

Marsha didn't move. She kept her eyes on Franck's face. It was the only part of him that was unbruised, unbroken. His body was translucent. The detective and the sergeant studied the effect.

"You can close it," she said. "And where is Nana?"

Sergeant Delvecchio moved to another drawer. Marsha and McDuff followed him. This time, he did not hesitate to pull the drawer open.

Marsha did not look down at the body at first, and then she did. It had the same veined, pale brown translucence as Franck's. Marsha's eyes followed the stitches along her grandmother's chest to her abdomen.

She started to breathe hard and fast. Her eyes watered and her chin trembled. Sergeant Delvecchio thought she was going to be sick. McDuff walked up behind her, to steady her. As soon as he touched her elbow, her knees buckled.

"I've got you," he said, holding her around the waist.

Marsha held her head. She was shrieking. She struggled to turn around, to throw her arms around McDuff's neck for support, but her legs wouldn't carry her.

He was at the door, almost out of the room, dragging her. McDuff was surprised at how heavy she was.

"Shut it–shut it," he kept saying.

Sergeant Delvecchio, head down, shut the drawer.

It was the last time he would see the old woman's or Franck's body. By morning, before the funeral home arrived to claim them, they both disappeared from their vaults.

39

"So you could fly."

"Yes."

"I ain't surprise. You always been different." Sashanna hugged her legs closer to her chest and stuck her chin in the air. "It one reason I love yuh."

He didn't look up when she said this, but he watched her out of the corner of his eyes. He didn't say anything, either, because he realized they had always loved each other, and it seemed such an obvious declaration, now. Instead, David listened to her, observing his own ground rules. She could ask him anything, and he would answer honestly, he told her–no matter how unbelievable or hurtful the truth. No more duppy-dust deception.

David had already flown Sashanna four times up and down the moss-covered face of the coral ridge where they went hiking. Each time, she closed her eyes and giggled, thrilled and terrified. The way she was on the Swinging Boat at Coney Island the last time the travelling amusement park came to Barbados.

"You've a great gift, David. Yuh know?"

"Uh-huh," he said, making it sound more like a statement than the doubting question it was.

"Yes," Sashanna said. "Most people dream uh dem lives meanin somethin, mekkin a difference. You know it so, every time yuh fly." She smiled at him for the first time since they began to talk.

"It's not so simple, Sashanna," he said.

"How yuh mean? From wha you tell muh, all wunnuh gotta do is stand up fuh Buhbaydus–"

"We don't know who or what we'll be going up against. I've never been in a fight in my life. You know that."

"But you could *fly.*"

"Maybe they can, too."

"And yuh won't be alone."

"Right now, I am. Milton can't or won't help me. Marsha's MIA. And without Franck, it doesn't matter what decision I'd make."

"No," she said, standing up. She went over to where he was standing. "You *ain't* alone."

She put her arms around him. He touched his forehead to hers, stroked the scar on her cheek.

"De truth, David?"

He nodded.

"I ain't wan you tuh die, an if uh know for certain yuh would, uh would tell Milton you ain't goan nowhere wid he. But I want yuh do dis, David. I want yuh tuh do wha's right."

Sashanna started to cry. She turned her head away. "You must tink uh foolish, bewitched by all dis obeah...."

He held her face in his hands, steadied her. "No," he said. "You always been the practical one... it one of the reasons I love you, too."

She buried her chin in his chest. He held her close to contain his own tears.

"Uh doan want yuh to die...."

"Nobody wants to die–"

The cellphone on his hip vibrated.

"Yes?"

"David. It's me. Marsha."

He hadn't checked the number. He thought it might be Milton.

"I tried to reach you at home," she said.

"I'm out with Sashanna."

"Good, good. Hey, listen–"

"Where are you?" he said.

"I'm still in Montreal... don't worry, I comin home.... But listen, boy... I frighten. I mean, real, real frighten. We ain't talkin bout a small fight, here, some bassa-bassa or Cantina, *High Noon* brawl, which I could handle.... David, Franck's.... Tell Milton Franck was right bout the Lodge... it ain't no trick... them ain't playin. The Heart Man get he, David, get he *real* good. He nearly had me, too–" She took a deep breath.

"Marsha? Are you sure? Are you sure Franck's...?"

She exhaled. "Boy... bout as sure as I can be of anythin right now. Why?"

"Something Milton said when we spoke. But are you–?"

"I'm OK... tryin *hard* tuh be.... I din call you long distance on yuh cell tuh bawl again.... I just want you to know I sorry, man, I can't tell yuh how sorry I is... but I comin back, now.... I comin home. And maybe stayin out here in this cold place would be de best thing for muh tail right now, Heart Men or no, but–" There was another deep breath. This time her voice returned steadier and stronger: "Nana died protectin me not just *from* somethin but *for* somethin... somethin greater than myself... there, I said it; Lord help me.... The least I can do is see what in the world de old woman was thinkin."

"Do you think Milton's right?" said David quickly, before she hung up. "About us?"

"Lord, I ain't know," she said, exhaling loudly again, "but all I can tell yuh is I comin.... I comin home."

40

"You're leaving us?" he said, walking across the parking lot to where she stood outside the reception office.

Marsha had seen when McDuff pulled up and waited to meet him. She held a brown envelope in her right hand. Her duffle bag was over her left shoulder. She shielded her eyes as he approached, sensitive to the glare of the cold midday sun. "I've already called a taxi. Save you the trip. You said it: I don't belong here."

McDuff nodded. "But it's more than that. You've made up your mind."

"About some things, yes. About others...." She handed him the envelope.

"What's this?"

"A number. Call me later–if you can."

"When? Where am I calling?"

She smiled. "You're the detective. You'll figure it out."

McDuff put the envelope in his jacket's inside pocket. "The Heart Man said he was under the protection of the Circle of the Grand Order." He watched her. "I've never had any direct dealings with them, but I know of them. They're supposed to be good people, Marsha, honourable. But maybe something has happened there, too... to the inner column."

"They're powerful. Right?"

"Yes. They'd have to be to harbour someone like the Heart Man for so long."

"I thought Milton and Mackie were bad enough," she said. "What do *they* want?"

"The same thing every society gone bad wants."

"Which is?"

"A world of their own making."

McDuff held his arms close to his sides, hands in pants pockets. Marsha looked away and grunted. When she finally spoke, "I've seen some of that world," she said, meeting his eyes. "It ain't for me, either."

41

"Tek dat!" cried one of the men, slamming hard the plywood table. The dominoes shook out of alignment, and his partner placed his card at the end.

"Yeah? Yuh tink so? Yuh *tink* SO?" *Bram.* His card crashed the others. The table jumped. "How bout *dat!*"

Both men looked to a third player, who studied her hands.

".... I cahn play," she said, shaking her head.

"How yuh mean?" said First Man.

"Play, man, play," said Second Man.

"You done block de game."

"Wha?" said Second Man.

"You ain't know how tuh count?" said First Man.

Third Man, the woman, whistled low. "The man block de game, den, an he ain't even know...."

They all lay down their cards, showing their hands. They started to debate what was played and at which point in the game.

Milton passed the men and woman, now drinking and laughing and shuffling the dominoes, just outside the entrance to De Gateway Café.

Dominoes, he was learning to appreciate, apart from the loud cussing and self-made behaviour it stirred, was as gloriously uncertain in outcome as their coveted cricket, played just down the road at the century-old Kensington Oval, once described as a West Indies fortress during the team's triumphing days. With that thought, and a single step, Milton walked onto the middle of the darkened pitch, which reminded him of the Coliseum or an Elizabethan playhouse; then he heard Mackie from across the island in the east, and he was there, too. While he was searching the grounds of a field where Barbadians used to stage rebellion, his comrade was cutting through terrain where one was actually waged.

Milton felt the restless spirits in the stands overlooking the pitch and of those in the soil of the cane field where Mackie stood. Tonight he missed the warmth of the stars, ever clouded. Mackie was right: the Elect were taking too long this time.

"Even if taking your time ain't laziness, Milton, they are more reckless than ever. And now you tell me there's evidence elements of the Circle of the Grand Order *are* involved. I still don't feel their presence."

"They've masked their movements well."

Mackie poked the earth with a cane stalk. He turned up clumps of grey mud studded with brown-and-white coral stones. Milton listened. The fields around them were dark and hushed, except for the faint rattle caused by the wind. There were fewer safe places for them with the beasts about.

"They think he died here, you know."

Milton's eyes narrowed. He was about to ask a question then opened his thoughts: "I know," he said. "1816. Both victor *and* vanquished preferred the African dead."

"How many times have we been through this? And do they *ever* get it right?" Mackie stabbed at the ground.

Milton listened. Because of their number of incarnations, neither one of them could say for certain.

"They only have to get it right this once, Machiavelli."

"He had a wife, a family, children whose descendents now sit in their legislature."

Milton nodded.

"They think he died during the revolt. He survived his captors. He lived in exile among his own people until his death, in a field not far from here, years later."

"Machiavelli...."

The Elder buried his cane stalk to the hilt with a grunt. His eyes crackled.

"But you can *feel* what happened here. His blood–their blood–is in the soil, courses through this coral earth."

"*We* can feel it. You know it is not so easy for them–"

"To what? Tell the truth?"

Milton approached his comrade, put his hand on his shoulder. "To tell it, you must first be able to see it. They can't, not always, at first."

Mackie didn't shrug him off. "They won't fight," he said.

"Not yet." Milton dropped his hand, sighed. "One still missing, one gone... one unsure."

"My charges have been ready for some time. They don't want to save the world. They just want to fight for it." He paused. "Do you think the old ladies would tell you anything more?"

This time, Milton knew who he meant. "I didn't want to push it, after our encounter."

"Maybe you should."

42

Milton walked up the steps to the obeah women's dwelling. At the other end of the verandah, there was a wicker-back mahogany rocking chair. He scanned the thick bushes surrounding the property, to see if anything was watching or had followed him. When his eyes returned to the verandah, Black Cat was sitting in the rocking chair.

"Shouldn't you be in school?" she said, staring him down.

"Shouldn't you *not* be talking to me?"

Black Cat took her eyes off him and eased back in the chair with her stick. She began to rock and smile slowly.

"You're a brave one."

Milton was puzzled by the statement.

"So is the other–what do you call yourselves?–Elder. But I don't like him."

It was Milton's turn to smile.

"And I'm not too fond of you, either."

"No?" Milton said.

After a pause, "You may as well sit," she said, and with a turn of her hand revealed another rocking chair made of the same mahogany and wicker as hers.

Milton was reluctant.

"Oh, don't be foolish. I won't bewitch you, though it'd be fun to try. Care for some cocoa tea?"

"No. Thank you."

She chuckled. He sat.

"What do you want?" she said.

"Your help." Before Milton could say the two words, Black Cat was shaking her head. He put up his hands, palms out. "To talk, then. We can do that."

Her sea green eyes grew small.

"I suppose. What do you want to talk about?"

"About how–when–we may have known each other."

Black Cat stopped smiling, stopped rocking.

"You would have to tell me."

Although she spoke the words clearly and directly, they surprised him. And she spoke again before he knew how to respond:

"I'm not like you, Elder–I'm not a manifestation of the current Cataclysm. Not a direct manifestation, as with you and your brother and my two sisters."

Milton followed her words closely. Sitting beside her, he studied the washed-out colour of her eyes and hair, her bulk and heavy breasts. She sweated. He smelt the warmth held by her body as if baked into the clay of her flesh. He could picture her as a wild child.

"You *are* human," he said.

"I thought you'd never notice."

"But that's–"

"Unlikely, not impossible. 'No more so than it is for an obeah woman to have been handsome, once.'"

"But how?"

"All right, Elder." Black Cat began to rock again. "No more silly subterfuge?"

Milton nodded, not quite understanding.

"They called me Mother Sally back in the day, though I would never have any children of my own. I was a midwife. A catcher, not a bearer, of babies."

"And of men?" Milton guessed.

She grinned, fully and openly. "I said I wasn't motherly."

"You did," said Milton. "So that is how we know each other?"

"Yes."

"For how long?"

"Not long. Not as humans understand it. We both looked different then. Though you were not much younger than you appear today. We first met in this house… before my father threw me out."

"I am sorry."

"For what? It took me years to figure out what I was freed for, but on that day I knew what I had been freed from."

"Was I… unkind to you?" Milton asked.

"You could be. Often, yes." She stopped rocking to gaze at him. The look was not scornful. "You were a man. And very much of that time."

"If I injured you in any way–"

"It has since been forgotten, I'm sure."

Black Cat and Milton stared at each other. Neither wanted to be the first to turn away.

"What do you want, Elder? Forgiveness for actions you no longer remember as your own?"

He said after a while: "Our situation–that of an Elder–is unusual. Unlike you, I exist without knowing fully who I was or the ability to appreciate who I might be. It's somehow… reassuring… someone remembers, and the memories are not entirely unpleasant."

Black Cat nodded. "Not entirely."

Milton rose to leave. She sat back in her chair.

"Thank you," he said and descended the short steps.

"Home drums beat *first*," she tossed at his back with a strike of her stick against the verandah's hard wood. Milton stopped and turned. She had a small smile. "Stay *close* to home."

Milton gave a short nod and waved to her then made his way to De Gateway Café.

43

Marsha stood inside the doorway to the neat board-and-shingle house. Wisps of cobwebs hung in the corners, and milky light dripped through the drawn curtains. The air was musty from months of being enclosed. A fine layer of salty dust coated the coffee table, dish cabinet, and mesh larder. Marsha breathed slowly, as if the slightest disturbance would cause the house to crumble and collapse. She had run, swift as an ocelot, from the ferry here, through cocoa and immortelle. She didn't care who saw her.

She wasn't sure what she would find.

The house was still standing. She felt a warmth in its four walls that had nothing to do with the shining sun or sea breeze.

The telephone rang. She picked it up.

"Hello."

"Hi. Marsha? It's McDuff. Julius."

"I know," she said with a smile. "You're on time."

"I was trying earlier but got no answer. Am I calling Tobago?"

"Yes. Nana's old place." She touched the cross around her neck and cleared her throat. "I'm looking for my Rosebud–any Rosebud."

"And how is it?" said McDuff.

Marsha sighed. "Still here. And, if you don't count the mummi-fied rat by the stove, much as she left it. The beets are soon ready. So are the bonavist. *Someone* must be watering her garden."

"That's good."

"It is."

"So you're all right."

Marsha sat in a comfortable chair her Nana used to drag to the kitchen table. There were scissors and white glue beside clippings on a placemat. She shuffled some with two fingers.

"What did you say?"

"All *right*," McDuff repeated.

The scraps of paper were recipes cut from assorted calendars and local magazines.

Marsha checked her watch. Shivered with a rush of heat. It was time to go, go back. If she wanted to save this place and maybe more than this place.

"Not yet," she said. "But almost there."

44

Mackie was pacing outside the entrance to De Gateway Café when Milton appeared. The hair on Mackie's head and arms bristled, his shoulders twitched. He was muttering to himself, back and forth, cussing. When Milton was a few feet from the entrance, Mackie threw up his right arm. Sparks flew from his eyes.

"Stop!" he shouted. "Or, Godblimuh, I'll incinerate you."

Walking headlong toward him, Milton barely deflected Mackie's bolt into the sea.

"*What* is wrong with you? If anyone saw–"

"Shut up," he said. Milton stood back, raised his other hand. There were beasts, like the soukouyan, that could assume the shape of others.

"Machiavelli...?"

"Where have you been?"

"Why? What's wrong?"

"What's 'wrong'? Come. Lemmuh show you."

Milton did not move.

"Come on, man," Mackie said. "And put down your hands before one of the patrons asks questions."

Milton followed him cautiously.

He sensed something in the establishment was different–out of place–or now in place... had sensed it upon his approach but didn't know how to interpret it. Until seeing what his comrade had seen and the sparks in his eyes.

And sometimes they does be feared, too.

"There is another?" he whispered without taking his eyes off the young man before him.

"Yes," Mackie nearly shouted.

"This is what Mother Sally meant about 'home drums.'"

"Who?"

"The obeah woman.... Did he now walk in?"

"Yes–no! I didn't notice him... at first. Milton, he's been sitting at the back of the rum-shop for the last three days."

"All this time," Milton said. "All this time." He looked at Mackie, who had yet to take his eyes off the young man. His comrade's shoulder's still twitched. "What's wrong with you?"

"Him," Mackie said, with a jolt of his chin. "He is not right... he is an aberration."

"But he *is* the one we've hoped for."

"Yes. *Another* saviour."

"Well, then."

Mackie took a step back, shook his head.

"We must talk to him, see if *he* knows...," Milton said.

"You first."

Milton walked over to where the young man sat. Closer to him, he could tell he was older than the Elect, already past twenty-one.

"Excuse me," Milton said. He stood beside his table. "May we join you a moment?"

The young man's stick, which neither Elder had seen below the table, flew up and Mackie stood in front of Milton, his hand raised. The tip of the stick nearly touched his palm.

The young man spoke. Deliberately, in a voice made up of many.

"'We hold no nation, by virtue of its might, as infallibly right in any conflict, nor do we mistrust any nation because of its size, wealth or power. We will be allies of all yet will be outposts to none.'"

The young man sat back. His expression relaxed. His stick lowered.

Milton stepped from behind Mackie to assess the scene. Some of the patrons and staff of the rum-shop had seen and heard their exchange. Sam and Cooper, who had made up in the back seat of his car, came closer. Johnny and his art, far from either one's thoughts right now, were still missing. "Mackie," Milton warned his comrade, tilting his head toward him.

Mackie slowly lowered his hand.

"We apologize," Milton began.

"Don't dig nothin," the young man said.

"I'm Milton. This is Mackie. What's your name?"

"K–" the young man said. He stuttered to find his words. "Ka… Kah… um… uh… Kah… uhh… um… uh…."

"Kai," said Mackie. "You are Kai. Where did you come from?"

At the mention of a name, the young man stop puzzling over whether or not it was his. "Skipper," he said in a clear, local voice, "somethin tell muh tuh be here. So I's here."

Milton looked up at the ceiling then down at the floor as if considering Kai's reply. He turned to leave.

"Where are you going now?" Mackie called after him.

"To find David," he said. "Marsha's returned."

"Who–?"

"The *strong one.*"

"Then we've got them all?" he shouted.

"We've got them all," Milton cried back. "Again."

Marsha and David wouldn't let go. They had been holding hands silently since she cleared customs, and she went to him and Sashanna waiting for her beyond the exit doors.

"I'm so sorry," he said. "If we had known…."

She told him again what had happened; to Franck, Nana, herself, and in telling it found she couldn't stop crying.

Sashanna came up beside them and rubbed Marsha's bare arm. Marsha wore a red tank top and black track pants. Aside from her duffle bag, she looked like she had come fresh from home. "Hey," Sashanna said, "dat muh man yuh wettin up so."

Marsha raised her head from his left shoulder. David's blue polo shirt was stained with tears. "Sorry... sorry...," she said. "You're right."

"That's better." Sashanna tried to give Marsha's arm a gentle squeeze. "You strong, girl... and *tall.*"

Marsha wiped her eyes and laughed.

"We gine figure it out," Sashanna said.

Marsha noticed the way Sashanna watched them both: with open love for David and in wonder at her.

"Yes, uh done know de story," she said before Marsha could ask David. "And wunnuh shall overcome."

David's cell rang. He stepped away to answer it. The conversation was brief.

"We've got to go," he said. He started to head for the car park and they followed.

"What's happened?" said Marsha. "Was that Milton?"

David nodded. "He wants us to come to De Gateway Café."

"How did he sound?"

"I don't know." David's eyes met Sashanna's over the top of the car. "Better than the last time we spoke?"

And yet something troubled him, and Marsha, too. They looked toward the east, together and at the same time. Nothing. A hot haze. Two houses flying flags for Independence. They had almost forgotten what day it was. Their minds briefly linked. I swore... I felt... a rumble... like an earthquake....

"What wunnuh waitin for? Christmas?"

They got in and headed for the highway.

Mackie sat across from Kai while Milton made his call. He shifted in his seat so that he faced the young man and no side of him was exposed.

Another saviour? Who had ever heard of such an occurrence? For all the Elders forgot, from one existence to the next, certain knowledge remained. All beings had their place and purpose. Not two or three. Only one. Kai could not be a saviour–because of what he had been–yet there he was, *in body.* For Mackie, it was like watching Uncle Sam or Union Jack come to life. It should not have been probable, yet Mackie had discovered these Bajans had a talent for improvisation that approached innovation.

"I can feel what you were. So can Milton–but he refuses to admit it."

"Because he needs me as I *am.*" It was not a question.

After a pause, "Yes," said Mackie.

"Look, all I know is wherever I need tuh be, somehow I does be. Simple so."

"No," said Mackie, "*not* so simple. How do we know for sure *you're* the one?"

Kai shrugged. "I's here."

"What are you, then?" He leaned into Kai, his eyes crackling.

"Skipper," he said, "I doan know if I can answer dat, but I can tell yuh what I been. I been the rockstone pon which de invaders landed and de salt Arawaks suck from de sea, I been de Caribs' shield in times uh war and de breadfruit offering in times uh peace, I been de little cane-piece de slaves plant and de sweetness de slave master grind outta she. I been explorer, legislator, colonizer, freedom fighter, and all the chains dem wear only to brek. I wear de flag and I been de flag. Industry made proud. De whip and de lash. Confessor and redeemer. Black and white an every redyellow mixupting in-between. Skipper, I been what my people need me to be in de best uh times and de worst, or whenever they does need me."

"You shouldn't be here—as you are now. You are an aberration—a freak of Nature."

"I ain't know bout that. I's here as real as you, as out uh place and part uh dis place as you. I's part of who have been, and of all what still are, the powerful and the powerless, them who can act and them who jus stand there, them inside me and them next to me."

"But you must not be destroyed," Mackie said, almost pleading.

"Should not," Kai corrected him. "*I* know wha happens if de spirit of a people dies."

Mackie peered into Kai's eyes. He saw something, felt it. Just a glimpse, but it was enough. The echo of an Elect was too strong to deny. That was why Kai seemed always to have been there, at the back of the bar... his essence so familiar they'd take him for granted, so reanimated they'd have to take notice of him.

And sometimes they does be fast, so fast you can't see them.

Mackie rubbed his eyes. "Boy," he said, "yuh still too hard ears. That spirit is not on trial, here."

Kai reclined in his chair. He thought about the Elder's words. "Since when?" he said, and with that neither had another word to say on the matter.

45

Baccous swarmed the rooftops while duppies flew to old haunts they once knew as soldiers, slaves, and salesclerks. The Hag belched balls of fire into storefront windows, and her cousin, La Djablès, hunted for living souls to consume. Everything Mr. Harding touched—stone, wood, iron—he burned.

Down Roebuck Street, Anansi as Lion and Steel Donkey ripped through parked cars. Dozens of duppies followed, like cockroaches erupting from a well. Shaggy Bear, a motley blur, pulled ahead of them. People scattered at Queen's Park. Panic spread to National Heroes Square in Broad Street, where the bank-holiday crowd sang and danced round Lord Nelson.

The baccous stopped to bang their stones slowly. The Bear threw up his arms. "There it is." Baccous punched holes into permaclad, slate shingles, galvanized sheeting, reinforced concrete. The Bear roared. The city shook to its coral foundations.

Then brother Neptune—dark as the deep and trident in hand—rose and crashed into the city with a tsunami.

46

The television was turned to the government channel before they lost reception. Everyone in De Gateway Café had been watching the report from Bridgetown. It wasn't clear what was happening. A group of costumed looters seemed determined to upstage the Independence Day celebrations. It was mas gone mad! Some were even seen scaling the treasury building where portraits of the nation's most loyal sons and daughters oversaw the event. The army was actually firing at them, and so were the police. Real bullets! Nuff bullets! People trampled each other, children sucked out of clinging arms were mashed underfoot. There were screams, bloody screams.

A big man dressed in a clownish suit of bristling fur pushed his face into the camera, growled at the sea. The cameraman swung around. The reporter, who had been doing her best not to lose it, whispered a curse. The sound of crushing waves mixed with gurgling laughter.

Snow swept away static lines, and soon there was nothing, a black screen.

Many outside the rum-shop were still facing south, where heavy wet smoke rose from the centre of the city like mini mushroom clouds. Marsha and David had arrived with Sashanna soon after the reporters dove into the conflict. Milton watched them come inside. There was fear in their eyes, sadness and anger, but none of the outrage or disbelief of hours before. Bridgetown was burning. Even when it was under water, the fire wouldn't out. Flames fanned up to a chorus of cackles.

"We're out of time," said Milton. "Whatever you three decide is your choice."

Kai rose from where he sat and approached the two, stick in hand.

"He should not go," said Mackie, pointing at Kai and loud enough for David and Marsha to hear.

But when Kai stepped beside them, all three shone: the way they had in the gully, when they first discovered their connection. Kai's thoughts became open to them, and theirs to him.

Sashanna stood away from them, gazing at their light. Although Cooper and Sam were caught in its arc, no one else in De Gateway Café seemed troubled by their glow. She turned to Mackie. He stood silent, arms at his sides.

We have tuh go, said Kai.

Try to help, said David.

What we waitin for, then? Marsha also spoke without speaking.

As he turned, David saw Sashanna's face. She rushed to hold him.

"I don't want to leave you," he said, keeping her close.

"Uh know."

"You should be safe here with Milton, and Mackie–"

She put her fingers to his lips. Sushed him. "Uh know. Is alright, everyting's gine be alright. Jus go." She stroked his cheek and kissed him. "Go be a hero."

When Kai, Marsha, and David were out the door and in the sky, Milton said only three words to Mackie before he disappeared from the rum-shop: "Prepare your charges."

47

Bridgetown had waited long to burn like this, on a slow fuse. It was the oldest city in the western hemisphere—over 370 years—where slaves were first brought and broken and sold, and from where the method for keeping chattel orderly, in chains even when there were none, had been perfected then exported to other colonies up and down the archipelago. Duppies who had died on the auction block exploded the boardwalk where they once were forced to stand. Runaway slaves who had burned with exposure and dried up from thirst in The Cage burst from the ground where their blood had oozed from the wire-and-wood prison into the earth below. This land was fertile ground: in every coral brick baccous gleefully dislodged, in the dark soil the Steel Donkey's hooves dug from the ground, in the sandbox and royal palm and baobab, resided the fears, dreams, riddims, and revolutions of conquered peoples who long ago thought of themselves as conquering. The city had felt fires before, over a hundred, two hundred, three hundred years ago, that left burnt-out districts worthy of a bombing, that consumed acres of wooden dwellings. The beasts were determined to make those conflagrations seem like the spark of small kindling in a steel drum.

"…. Too… many…. There are… too many of them!" cried David, rocketing past Marsha and Kai into a barrage of baccous wall high. He knocked them down, five, ten, fifteen at a time. They climbed back up. He toppled them to the ground; spinning, they bounced and rolled. Fixing wild red eyes on him, they shrugged and got up again, their skinned-teeth neither laugh nor smile.

The buildings that housed the third oldest Parliament in the New World were on fire, from east wing to west, back and front. In the courtyard, gangs of baccous stood howling, flaming rum bottles held high in greasy hands. Those above were peeling the roofing off the towers as if they were opening sardine tins. Up and down Broad Street, baccous were dismantling Cave Shepherd, Dacostas Mall, the Mutual Building, the Old Town Hall, hurling bricks with deadly ease into the streets, through windows and at each other, snorting and squealing as they knocked themselves clear across rooftops. After cousin Neptune's big wave, there were few humans left to crush. Mr. Harding cut through the last stand of soldiers and constables with a crack of his whip. Seaweed and fish and other dead ocean things smoked at his feet, the smell raw and briny. The Hag roasted anyone who tried to escape.

In the middle of Bridgetown, Marsha wrestled with the Bear. She bloodied her hands punching through his coral casing, and with a lash of his arm he cut open her back. She fell to her knees, plunged her fists into the ground. Even after the Heart Man, it was still unbelievable–*unacceptable*–that their blows could hurt her so. "Is that all you can take?" the Bear said. Marsha looked up at him with a growl. For all the Elders' obvious power and might, she may as well have been directed by Ingmar Bergman. The Bear hurtled toward her. She threw a left, hard and fast, and he swung up a massive paw. The walls shook, from the Lower Green to Baxter's Road.

David flew down Broad Street searching for survivors. Below him two men and a woman ran out of a store, stumbling over bodies washed out by the tsunami's retreat. The Steel Donkey burst through the display window. It trampled the two men first then the woman, stomping their heads into the ground. The beast stopped when it saw him. David pulled up at the traffic lights by Nelson's statue. The Steel Donkey was charging, gaining speed as if it meant to leap into the air after him. David froze. He didn't know if the beast could fly or not–

Kai appeared in its path. He lashed the beast with his stick, and it careened into a light pole. Without turning, he said, "Where's Marsha?"

"With the Bear."

"Does she need our help?"

"I hope not.... You'll be all right?"

Kai nodded, raising his stick.

David rose and flew in the direction of Queen's Park, where the leaves of an ancient baobab tree drooped with duppies.

"Come," said Kai. The Steel Donkey shook its helmeted head, stunned. "Yuh remember me, now?"

Its eyes shone smoke blue. It did.

Kai stood with his stick low, like a cricket bat. He let the beast rush past him. Cut up.

The beast howled.

It turned and reared on its hind legs. Kai stood, his stick raised. A gash in the beast's earthy armour oozed something oily. The beast snorted coal fire onto the pitch. Charged again.

But this time Kai knew something about it he didn't before. He held his stick high.

"Come, nuh," he cried.

A fiery brick struck the back of Kai's hand. His stick spun from him. A ring of baccous on the rooftops above cheered as the Steel Donkey bowled into him.

Kai grabbed its head with both hands before it hit him full in the chest. His hands started to shimmer, as if made of fine dust and hardly there. The stands of baccous stopped their cheering. The Steel Donkey's smoky blue eyes grew wide, alarmed.

Now the beast knew something about him it didn't before.

The Steel Donkey charged harder, intent on ploughing him into Nelson's statue. Kai put down his left foot, then his right. The beast slowed until Kai's back was against the warm marble plinth of the monument now roped in seaweed.

Kai held the beast's head and looked into its eyes. Before it could think what to do next, he wrenched his arms to the left.

The Steel Donkey's neck broke with a mechanical snap. Its body fell to the ground in a clatter.

Kai retrieved his stick. Baccous started to peer over the edges of rooftops along Broad Street. One began to beat a brick along guttering, then another, like spoon and pan....

Milton appeared before him.

"This is where the fight begins, not where it ends." He pointed to the sky, toward the grey centre of the island, where a storm had formed.

"How we gine stop this? They's too many. Baccous an Hag an beasts uh never knew could exist."

"Leave the baccous. Head for Mount Hillaby."

Kai frowned.

"What part David and Marsha?"

"They have seen me and heard me as you have."

Milton faded from sight. Kai nodded. He began to walk in the direction of Mount Hillaby, allowing himself to be drawn there, where he was meant to be, each step taking him closer to there, further from here, where he was, until he stood beneath the eye of the storm. A moment later, David flew above him. A moment more, Marsha ran to his side.

Together again, they began to shine. This time, they didn't stop.

48

David, Marsha, and Kai stood in a clearing. They were at the island's highest point, overlooking the greenest of fields outside of Scotland, which was how the district below them got its name. A grey swirl of wind and rain and dust churned above their heads, and they could see the shape of four figures in it. One looked like Mackie, the other three were also familiar but flickered as if by lightning. The Elect watched the dark reflections. They had to enter the eye of the hurricane, knew this when they arrived. As much as they didn't want to enter the hurricane, they were drawn to it. And they very much didn't want to enter it.

For all the baccous and Heart Men and Steel Donkeys they faced, nothing had filled them with greater dread than what they could barely see waiting for them in the sky.

They looked at each other and the thought occurred to all of them at once: "I don't want to die. Do you?" But there was no time to answer, not even in thought.

David rose between Marsha and Kai. They reached up; each held a hand. He lifted them into the hurricane until they were at its very heart.

And there was no sound. Of any kind.

Marsha and Kai let go of David's hands. They landed in mid-air, walked on water. Mackie's charges stood before them. They flickered, short-circuited. In that flash, the Elect recognized their opposite numbers, and the shadowy mirror images recognized them.

They raced toward each other.

There was no great struggle. No bloody blows or righteous words. Only a rush. A collision. Conflict. Flash of light. And two gone. The closer they drew together, they began to disintegrate, drop by drop, particle by particle. And another two gone. When they met, when they clashed, thunder burst the sky, lightning split the sea, the mountain moved and clouds trembled. And another two gone. Until there was none left except the first two and the rest of the world and rain fell across the island from North Point to South Point, from Ragged Point to Needham Point, soft and quiet as ash.

End of Part 3

FRIDAY, DECEMBER 21, 2001

She walks through lemon-grass and circe-bush, on a hill over-looking the sea. She passes a young man and young woman lying in each other's arms on a blanket, but she is gradually fading from this world. She passes them, gently as a country breeze, and with even less of a sound.

It's as if she has always been here, yet she can't recall when she came up or if she ever went down. She walks through the bush to the edge of a cliff. There are people on the beach below, many children and men along the shore. She hails the sun. She thinks: *I could stay up in here forever.* The next moment, she knows she will: stay up here, though not forever; until she is needed: by the couple on the blanket or the children on the beach or the fathers who care for them or any one of her people.

Papa-papa.... She turns her head. She sees the red and yellow flower of the island. She picks the flower, smells its nectar. She rubs its firm petals against her left cheek, staining it a sunset colour. Her name is now that of the flower, the flower's name is now hers. She keeps walking, then, fading. She feels: *Dis where uh meant to be... now... till....*

Everything dies.

Almost.

Mackie comes from the back of the courthouse. Milton is standing before the tower with a marble plaque embedded in it, a monument to the first settlers to the island.

"So it is finished," he says, hands in pockets. "Their world seems to be holding." He stands beside Milton, regarding the plaque.

"Yes. It is time for us, now," Milton says.

Mackie nods. "And what about the Circle of the Grand Order? If not for the fast one's Guardians, the Heart Man would have eluded us. Who knows how his mad presence would have played out."

"No," Milton says, "there's no doubt. Rogue elements in the Circle were using him as much as he thought he was using them. Maybe more so."

"Maybe more so," Mackie agrees. "What was he doing for them, though? Gathering strength?"

"Or seeking weakness. For the next time."

They both observe the plaque again. Its blackened letters gleam weakly in the sun.

"This is where it began," says Mackie.

"For them, yes. In 1605."

"So it reads…. I will miss this place, its people. Its beer. Even your other prodigals, Sam, Cooper and Johnny–they *were* strong, in the end."

"Only in the end?" says Milton. "'What all humanity knows, despite the success of our achievements or the scale of our aspirations, what shadows our acts and no less our feelings, is that we are only here for a time.'"

"From the Emissary?"

"Yes," Milton says, "for my last class–"

"Which you never did get to teach. You always try to give the game away, Professor."

"I didn't need to… this time."

"No," Mackie concedes. "They didn't need it, in the end. Save it. For the next time, then."

The doors and windows of the old chattel house are open. The rocking chair on the verandah whistles in the wind. There's a sign in the front yard, it reads in the shade of an evergreen:
FOR SALE BY OWNER
SERIOUS OFFERS ONLY.

The End

ACKNOWLEDGEMENTS

Sometimes after finishing a book, it feels as if there are too many people to thank; and you can never thank enough those you remember for the many, many ways, big and small, in which they contributed to your efforts. They lent their passion to your hope, helped you to create better, to be better, and not just as an artist.

I'd like to thank my former Graphic Design students at Barbados Community College Aguinaldo Belgrave, Joshua Clarke, Matthew Clarke, Richelle Durant, Kiel Hinds, Mario Knight, Neil Sorhaindo, and Tristan Roach, who asked, "Where are our heroes?" and whose quest to find them has inspired my own.

Things Fall Apart by Chinua Achebe, Richard Allsopp's *Dictionary of Caribbean English Usage*, *The Watchmen* by Alan Moore & Dave Gibbons, Marv Wolfman's *New Teen Titans* with George Perez, and Chris Claremont's *X-Men* circa John Byrne have long been companions on this journey, as well as Robert Cormier's uncanny fiction. Works by Barbadian writers and artists Addinton Forde, Patrick Foster, and Karen Lord have helped as well to temper and gird my own vision. I was also very fortunate to have John Wickham, whose life and work were the true inspirations for James "Jimmy" Weatherhead, as my emissary.

I remain very grateful to my Canadian publishers Keith Henderson and Steve Luxton of DC Books, and to Angela Leuck, their first line of defence, and Giuliana Pendenza, their able backup. Dear ladies, kind sirs, thank you for finding the work enjoyable and worthy of further pursuit.

There are allies and friends whose straight criticism, daily support, moral example, unselfish insight, casual enthusiasm, or faith in the

Bajan novel helped to make the completion of this book possible: Carolle "The Immortal One" Bourne, Micheal E. D. Bunn, Andie Davis, Linda M. Deane, Eugene Gibbs, Nailah Folami Imoja, Esther Jones, and Rommel Yearwood.

This story, over ten years in writing, owes much to family, too: my sister Shar, whose love of adventure stories prompted this one; my dad and his brothers, who told astonishing tales about Barbados, notably its stick fighters–true Bajan knights; my big brothers Cal and Pat, lifelong guardians and defenders; and my mom, from whom I learned about the Heart Man and obeah and more than we culture.

And very special thanks (again) to Sherry, the first one to read it, the first one to get it; and to Aeryn... so young yet already soaring beyond me.

RES, December 2012

Robert Edison Sandiford is the author of three short story collections, *Winter, Spring, Summer, Fall, The Tree of Youth* and *Intimacy 101: Rooms & Suites*; the graphic novels *Attractive Forces, Stray Moonbeams* and *Great Moves*; a travel memoir, *Sand for Snow: A Caribbean-Canadian Chronicle*; and edited with Linda M. Deane *Shouts from the Outfield: The ArtsEtc Cricket Anthology* and *Green Readings: Barbados, The First Five Years (2008-2012)*. He is a founding editor of *ArtsEtc: The Premier Cultural Guide to Barbados* (artsetcbarbados.com), and has worked as a journalist, book publisher, video producer with Warm Water Productions, and teacher. He has won awards for both his writing and editing, including Barbados' Governor General's Award of Excellence in Literary Arts and the Harold Hoyte Award, and been shortlisted for the Frank Collymore Literary Award. He still divides his time between Canada and Barbados.